Cold Winter's Kill

Special Limited Edition

99 of 200 copies

FIRST EDITION

Jeff + Susan!
Enjoy!
Bob Doerr

Cold Winter's

Kill

Bob Doerr

TotalRecall Publications, Inc.
United States   Canada   United Kingdom

All rights reserved. Printed in United States of America, Europe and Canada, simultaneously. Except as permitted under the United States Copyright Act of 1976, No part of this publication may be reproduced, stored in a retrieval system, or transmitted in any form or by any means electronic or mechanical or by photocopying, recording, or otherwise without prior permission of the publisher.
Exclusive worldwide content publication / distribution by TotalRecall Publications.

Copyright © 2010 by Bob Doerr

ISBN: 978-1-59095-762-2

This is a work of fiction. The characters, events, views, and subject matter of this book are either the author's imagination or are used fictitiously. Any similarity or resemblance to any real people, real situations or actual events is purely coincidental and not intended to portray any person, place, or event in a false, disparaging or negative light.

Printed in the United States of America with
simultaneously printings in Canada, and
United Kingdom.

1 2 3 4 5 6 7 8 9 10

FIRST EDITION

To all the men and women, past and present, who served their country in the Air Force Office of Special Investigations.

PROLOGUE

She struggled to regain consciousness. The biting cold helped but the residual drugs in her system encouraged her to go back to that peaceful quiet sleep. She knew she was in danger and was aware that now outside, no longer a captive in that awful house, that she had to make her move to escape. Soon it could be too late.

She pushed herself to her feet, the blowing snow temporarily blinding her in the evening darkness. Suddenly, she felt his hands grab her from behind.

"No! No!" Her screams swallowed instantly by the raging wind.

She half ran and was half pushed away from the hands on her back. She had only taken four or five steps when the ground disappeared under her feet and she realized she was falling. Her body slowly turned and rolled in the air. She looked back up into the snow now falling more slowly than she was.

The impact with the ground was surprisingly not as painful as she had expected. Maybe the heavy snow cushioned the fall. She tried to move and realized her limbs wouldn't respond. Perhaps she just needed a few minutes rest. Amazed at how peaceful she now felt, she stared up at the falling snow. The blowing wind did not reach down here. Even in the darkness the snow was beautiful and her mind drifted to thoughts of her family, her sisters. Death came before the snow had fully covered her.

Chapter 1

Just six hours ago I had received a phone call from John Ribbons, a friend of mine whom I had known for years and served with in the military. His youngest child, Melissa, had been on a ski trip with friends at Ski Apache. Two days ago she left her friends at the lodge to take a bus into Ruidoso to do some shopping and had not been seen since. I didn't want to say yes to John, but there was no way I could have said no. I didn't want to be making this drive. I remembered Melissa too well. She was a cute, sweet kid. I also knew that people who went missing in the Rockies in December usually turned up dead. I knew there could be a number of other better possibilities, but the odds worried me and I didn't want to be there when they found her.

John and his family lived in Florida. He had been in touch with the New Mexico State Police and Sheriff's office but nothing had materialized about Melissa's whereabouts. He was worried, but due to some important job related reasons John couldn't leave Florida for a few more days. So he called me and asked if I could drive down and see what I could find out. John reminded me of our fishing trip when Melissa used my fishing pole for the whole trip and I had to use her little one. He didn't need to remind me.

The sky was a deep black and the large bright moon was just setting over the Rockies. Driving alone this late in such a setting usually put me in awe of nature. Invariably I would be wishing I wasn't alone. The moon can be quite amazing here in the high desert, even quite romantic, but not tonight.

No, tonight I could feel that tug of Mother Nature, but my mind was full of concern and worry. What put me on Highway 70 between Roswell and Ruidoso, New Mexico, wasn't anything good. I drove on in the lonely darkness as the moon disappeared behind the mountain tops.

Ruidoso is rarely a very lively town and as I drove into it at one AM on a Thursday in December, the whole town looked as though it had been locked up tight. Street lights flickered and stop lights blinked on and off, but not much else showed any signs of life. My ultimate destination was Nocelo, a small town just west of Ruidoso's city limits. But I already knew there were no hotels in Nocelo, no police force, and nothing open at this time of night. I was just hoping someone was still awake to check me in at the Brown Bear Inn. I had called the receptionist at the Inn and told her that I would be late getting to Ruidoso. She told me not to worry. I did anyway.

I felt lucky to find any room available at such short notice in Ruidoso, a vacation town in the Capitan Mountains of New Mexico. This was the beginning of ski season and lodging was tight. I would have liked to have stayed at the Inn of the Mountain Gods, but it was booked solid. The few chain hotels were also full. One of the clerks I spoke to had recommended the Brown Bear Inn.

I found the Inn at the intersection of Highway 70 and Mescalero Drive, just where it was supposed to be. The bank next door had a sign out front that flashed the temperature among other irrelevant pieces of information. It was seven degrees Fahrenheit. Too cold for me and I couldn't help but think too cold for Melissa if she was outside somewhere.

The front door to the Brown Bear Inn was locked. I shook it hard to make sure the door wasn't just stuck, but it was locked. Stepping back I could see the bolt fastening the two doors together. I was thinking about walking around to look for another entrance when I saw movement inside. A short, elderly man in overalls and a bright red flannel shirt approached the door from the inside and opened it.

"Come on inside before you freeze," he said with a smile. "Are you Mr. West?"

"Yes, I am," I replied, a little surprised he knew who I was.

With a little twinkle in his eyes he followed up with a "Thought so."

"Hope you still have a room for me," I remarked as I followed him to the counter.

"Sure do, one of our finer rooms." I couldn't tell if he was pulling my leg. Actually the Brown Bear Inn looked as though it had seen better days, so I was already hoping my room would at least be comfortable. I wasn't expecting extravagant.

"Room 131, corner room, first floor, just down the short hall right behind us." He gave me the electronic key card and processed my credit card. "You'll need the key to get into the building after ten at night, but as you'll need the key to get into your room anyway, I suggest you keep it with you at all times. Do you need any help with your luggage?"

"No thanks," I responded and went back outside to get my one suitcase. It was beginning to snow. I was happy it waited for me to get here before it did. The sign at the bank said the temperature was still seven degrees.

I went back in. I guess because it had a name like the Brown Bear Inn, I was hoping the hotel might have some atmosphere. It had very little. The furniture in the lobby was plain, just a few chairs and a couch made of what I thought was brown naugahyde. The walls were pretty much bare. Fortunately, my room was fine. The heating system was working well and the shower had both hot water and enough water pressure to make taking a shower worthwhile. After my shower I went straight to bed. It had been a long day, it was late and I was tired. Usually I would have tossed and turned for some time, planning my next day's activities and thinking unpleasant thoughts about what may have happened to Melissa. But not tonight, the bed was comfortable and almost immediately after laying down I fell asleep.

In fact sleep came on so quickly, I was startled when I heard the blare of a truck horn and opened my eyes to see a sunlight filled room. The alarm clock said it was eight o'clock.

Sitting up in bed I studied the room. There wasn't much to it, a dresser, a small table with a chair and the bed. The rug was old and worn. There was a mirror on the wall over the dresser and a picture of a brown bear hung over the table. I wondered if all the rooms had the same picture hanging in them. Nothing to write home about but it had all I needed, a bed and a private bathroom.

After shaving, I got dressed and left my room in search of coffee. There was none in the room. I could smell it in the lobby but the pot must have been behind the counter in the office. The old man from the night before had been replaced by a woman, maybe a little younger than him, mid-sixties perhaps more. She was wearing an oversized brown sweat shirt that said Brown Bear Inn on the front. Her close cropped hair had a slight pinkish tinge to it.

"Good morning. Where's the best place to get a cup of coffee, maybe a couple eggs around here?" I asked the receptionist, hoping she might even offer me a cup of the Inn's coffee.

"Right across the street at the Mescalero Café." She nodded her head in the direction, I supposed, of the café.

"Thanks." I began walking towards the hotel door.

"Are you Mr. West?"

I stopped, turned and told her yes.

"Thought so. The Sheriff wants you to call him first thing. Might want to do it before you get your coffee."

I mumbled an okay, but didn't have any real intention of letting the Sheriff get in the way of my coffee. I walked out the door and crossed Highway 70 to the Mescalero Café. The snowfall had been light and it looked like we were going to have a nice sunny day. I took a chair in the empty café that faced the window giving me a view of the traffic going by on Highway 70.

A lady that I swear could have been the hotel receptionist's twin sister came up to take my order. I asked for coffee and some wheat toast. She walked back and relayed my order to another woman whom I couldn't quite see behind the counter. Rather than wait for the order she came back to me.

"Did Rose send you over?" She asked.

"If Rose is the lady at the Inn across the street, then yes."

"She's my sister. Gives us a lot of business. Where are you from?" She asked.

I usually don't mind talking to waitresses, clerks, anybody in the service profession. Their jobs can be menial and I like to be nice. But I could see my coffee being set on the counter behind her and really wasn't in the mood this morning for chit chat.

"Clovis," I responded. "Just down here for a bit of business."

"What kind of business are you in?" She asked, impervious to my coffee cooling behind her.

"Kind of a private contractor, just have a short assignment to do down here." I didn't want to discuss Melissa with her and I could see that my toast had arrived next to my coffee.

"Daisy, come get the man's order before it gets cold!" shouted the lady behind the counter. I couldn't see her but I instantly thought she was a beautiful and saintly person.

As Daisy walked towards the counter I wondered if all the kids in her family were named after flowers. I also turned and looked back out onto the road and noticed my view had been partially blocked by a Sheriff's sedan parked just outside the window. No one seemed to be in it.

At just that moment the café door opened and in walked a very young Sheriff's Deputy all decked out in his pressed uniform, shiny shoes and hat. He took just one step inside looked at me and asked, "Are you Mr. West?" I said I was and he continued, "Thought so, Rose said you might be over here. Mr. West, I need you to come with me right away. The Sheriff wants to talk to you."

"Can I drink my coffee first?" Daisy was standing next to my table, coffee in hand. "I'd be happy to buy you a cup, too."

"No sir," replied the Deputy. "I don't mean to be rude but the Sheriff has to leave town this morning and he told me to find you and get you to the station ASAP. We've got good coffee at the station."

Despite the aggravation, I did want to talk to the Sheriff

too. If he was leaving town then there was no use fighting the situation. I said okay and stood up to follow the Deputy out of the restaurant.

I guess in a way to mollify me, he turned to Daisy and said to put the breakfast on the Sheriff's tab. In turn, she grunted. I imagined the Sheriff kept one of those tabs that rarely if ever got paid off.

"Sorry about your breakfast Mr. West," the Deputy said once we were in his vehicle. "But the Sheriff was really specific about getting you picked up and delivered to him as quickly as possible. He is leaving town. I think he and his wife are going on a trip somewhere."

Great, I thought to myself, wishing I had just grabbed the coffee as we walked out. My mood didn't get any better as we drove right out of town on Highway 48 heading north. I asked Deputy Peter Blanco, he had identified himself as we drove away from the café, where the Sheriff's office was. I thought Ruidoso was the county seat.

"In Carrizozo, the county seat for Lincoln County," he responded. "It's only about a half an hour from here. You'll like the drive."

I resigned myself to the trip and did, in fact, enjoy the drive. It was very scenic and the route took us right through Nocelo. I had never been to Nocelo so it was good to get a feel for the small town before talking to the Sheriff. Describing it as small may be overstating its size. Nocelo was almost non-existent. A small collection of seven or eight buildings alongside the road and a couple of houses and other buildings set back from the road made up the whole town. Situated about eight miles northwest of Ruidoso on Highway 48, I wondered how in the world Melissa ended up finding a place to stay there.

Chapter 2

The road to Carrizozo took us around the foot hills that serve as the base for Sierra Blanco, a beautiful towering peak that tops off around twelve thousand feet above sea level. The day was sunny and clear, accentuating the natural beauty of the country around us. The terrain flattened out the last eight miles into Carrizozo.

Deputy Peter Blanco was a good chauffeur and seemed to be a pleasant enough guy. He pointed out some of the sights and freely answered my questions about how and why he ended up in law enforcement. He was from the small town of Capitan and had attended two years of college at Western New Mexico University. After obtaining enough credits for an Associates Degree from the University, he dropped out of school to find a job that would allow him to financially support his mother and father. His family was very poor and had sacrificed all they had to help him stay in college for the two years. Leaving college had been hard but Peter knew the Lincoln County Sheriff's office was looking for Deputies and he had always wanted to be a policeman. It had worked out well. He was hired, was making enough money to share it with his parents and was even able to take some night classes towards a full college degree. With luck he thought he would have enough credits to graduate in the summer.

He described the law enforcement workload in the

county as being light and rewarding. The county encompassed a lot of territory but not much in the way of population. Most of what the Sheriff's office did was help people with problems or minor emergencies. Sure, he admitted, there was crime, but mostly fights and disorderly conduct. Usually those incidents were caused by people drunk and more often than not by the same groups of people over and over.

Peter said he wasn't married yet but he did have a steady girl. He thought after he finished his degree, they might get engaged. I wished him luck. I meant it. He seemed like a good guy.

Carrizozo appeared to be no bigger than Ruidoso. The Sheriff's Office was a nice looking building located just inside the city limits. It looked just a couple years old, designed in what I call the old Southwestern motif, stucco buildings with red tile roofs. The landscaping, mostly xeriscape, was attractive and well taken care of. We parked around back and walked through a private entrance that took us into the Sheriff's personal waiting area.

A lady, not in uniform, looked up and smiled at Peter.

"Is this Mr. West?" she asked Peter. He nodded and she turned her glance towards me. She was a very attractive woman, maybe thirty years old, dark hair and dark eyes.

"Mr. West, please come with me, the Sheriff is waiting for you." I would have followed her without the please. She wasn't as tall as me, six feet, but she was close. She led me into the adjacent office and announced my presence to the Sheriff as we walked in.

The Sheriff was a tall, thin man. I guessed he was a few years older than me, but then I've been accused of forgetting that I was still aging too. He motioned to a chair next to his desk for me to sit in, but then walked back out of the room with his receptionist. Something about the way he put his hand on her back and talked to her made me think she was more than just another civil servant. They stopped just outside the door. I could hear him discuss some problem with his appointments for the following week. After maybe thirty seconds he turned and came back into the room closing the door behind him.

I stood up and shook his hand as he approached. He had a strong grip and used it, obviously to make an impression. I started to introduce myself but he cut me off. "Jim West, I know. I also know why you are down here. Mr. Ribbons called me and said you were coming down. I told him it wasn't necessary. I also checked you out. About this Melissa girl, sad thing, but it happens almost every year. Mother Nature is unforgiving. We have more people killed by the elements each year than we do by car accidents or murder. Two or three get lost outside at night each year and die. Four to ten die in their own homes and cabins when they lose power and don't have the sense to head for town. Three years ago we had a whole family of six freeze to death when their RV went off the road in a blizzard and skidded down the bottom of a ravine. Why they thought they could just stay in the RV and someone would find them we'll never know. No one knew they were missing. I figure they only lasted 36-48 hours. Hell they were only four miles from a town they must have driven through shortly before the accident. Forgive my rambling, Mr. West, I do feel sad for the Ribbons' family and I hope the daughter has just run off with some guy, but if she is out there somewhere, she is buried under the snow. Another cold winter's kill that we will not find until the spring thaw."

Obviously the Sheriff was not much into small talk. I knew what he was saying as it was what I had already concluded, but I felt obligated to justify my coming into his turf. "I imagine you're right Sheriff, but it can't hurt to go through the motions in an effort to at least determine if she has run off with some guy."

Although not my intent, perhaps calling him Sheriff jogged his sense of propriety, "Sorry, I never introduced myself, my name is Mike Mendez, call me Mike. Jim, you are welcome to do all the digging you want as long as you don't harass any of my citizens down here. I do really hope the young lady is safe."

"I can't imagine how I would harass anyone in your county, Mike. The Ribbons just wanted someone here on scene who they can talk to as much as they want about anything that comes to their mind at any hour they want. They know you can't give them that kind of priority. They just want to be reassured that everything possible is being done to find her." I knew as soon as the words came out of my mouth, that he didn't like something that I said. Although I had not meant to say anything to aggravate him, his lips drew back and his nostrils actually flared a bit as he leaned towards me. I figured he probably wasn't going to tell me to sit down, relax and stay a while.

"Listen, Mister, if you think you can come down here and disparage this office or the work we do, you better get out of my county and get out fast. I know all about you and how you like to sensationalize things in the press. We don't need you or the press making any more out of this than it is and I certainly don't need anyone libeling this office or the work that we do."

Give him credit. He had me speechless for a few seconds.

I had no idea where he was coming from or what he was referring to. Finally I threw back at him the only intelligent comment I could think of. "What in the world are you talking about?"

I don't know if it was dealing with crooks and liars for so long or what, but Sheriff Mendez didn't ease up a bit. "I'm referring to the murder case up in Denton a few years back and the child abuse case earlier this year in Ft. Sumner. It appears to me, West that everywhere you go the press shows up. We don't have a crime here; we have a missing person case. That is all. We don't need you and your friends in the press making something more out of it. Understand?"

"I don't."

"Understand?" he asked again, somewhat calmer, but just as pointedly.

"Yes." I replied. I would have continued but again he cut me off.

"Mr. West, I have to leave town for a few days. I have asked Deputy Blanco, the young gentleman who drove you here, to help you out in anything you need, within reason." He emphasized these last two words. "But if I get any idea you are trying to turn this into some scandal, you will be sorry. Do you get my drift?"

"I do, but your concerns are not warranted."

Again he cut me off. "I have to go now. Detective Blanco should be waiting in the outer office to drive you back to your hotel." He gestured to the door. I was being dismissed, so I left. Part of me was boiling and I wanted to do or say something, but my larger part was acknowledging that in my life I had been yelled at more harshly and dismissed more rudely than this. You have to accept it if you are going to go through life sticking your nose into what other people think is their business.   Many relationships start off like that and turn quite positive, others never do.   It was just life, and in life it is hard to avoid ego and ignorance.

Detective Blanco stood up when I came out of the office. "You ready, sir?"

I said I was and we walked out the private entrance. The receptionist was nowhere to be seen.

Chapter 3

"Where to?" Peter asked as we pulled out of the parking lot.

"Is there any place to get coffee in Nocelo?" Despite Sheriff's Mendez irrational outburst, there was no reason to not get started in what I came here to do. The last thing I had any interest in doing was contacting the press.

"No, I don't think there is. Not much in Nocelo at all. How about if we go back to that café and have breakfast on the Sheriff?" Peter had a conspiratorial grin on his face.

"Good idea," I smiled back at him.

"I couldn't help but hear your conversation with the Sheriff." Peter remarked. I felt like asking what conversation, but I held back.

He continued, "Sheriff Mendez is really not a bad guy. It's just there is an election coming up this year and he is in for another tough race. He barely won last time over the former Sheriff whom he had replaced the election before. I wasn't with the Office for the last election but I heard Sheriff Mendez gets all uptight the closer it gets. Maybe we just had the beginning of all that today. There is no love lost between former Sheriff Bass and Mendez."

"Well, if it is any consolation to you, Peter, I've never met or spoken to Bass and I have no interest whatsoever in bringing the press into this matter. I'm just trying to help an old friend find his daughter. My gut tells me your Sheriff is right, Melissa probably won't be found until the snows melt in the spring. I just don't want to give up hope and would like to be able to tell her family that everything has been done to find her. As you heard, I didn't get a chance to ask your Sheriff what investigative steps your department has already accomplished."

"Luckily you're riding with the right man. I handled most of the investigation myself. Maybe that's why they made me your point of contact. In addition to doing all the normal things done in any missing person case, like indexing her in all the state and federal data bases, I talked to everyone that remotely knew her in the whole county. No one had any idea what happened to her. She just vanished."

"Were there many people in the county whom she knew?' I asked.

"Actually no," replied Peter. "Other than the two friends who came with her, there were only four or five other folks who could remember talking to her. I'm sorry to say this Mr. West, but I don't think she ever left this county. Some people have theorized that she may have run off to California with some guy, but I couldn't find a shred of evidence to support such a possibility."

"Sounds like you did a good job, Peter. I am not here to second guess anything that you did." I wanted to stay on Peter's good side. I would need him to support my walking through all the same steps he had already taken. "If you don't mind I might talk to a few of those you have already interviewed."

"No problem, Mr. West, but her friends left town yesterday. Nobody else could provide me with anything worthwhile."

I was worried about that. "By chance did they give you a

phone number where they could be reached?"

"Absolutely, I have them in the case file in the trunk." Peter said this in a tone that implied that he might be young but he was no rookie.

"Good," I responded. I could see that we were now approaching Nocelo. "Which building did Melissa and her friends stay in?"

Rather than say anything immediately, Peter slowed the car down and turned left onto a narrow paved road that led to a series of three similar looking buildings about a quarter mile off the road.

"In the one on the right. Second floor, right hand side." He pointed as he said this. "All three of these buildings are owned by some rich guy from Texas. Each one has two apartments downstairs and two upstairs. They are all alike. I've never met the owner. I don't think he has been out here for years. He rents the apartments out all year round. They are usually never all full, except for the height of the ski season. You want to see one?" All three buildings were dull in appearance. Painted gray, the two story complexes could have passed for upper class, college dorms.

"Maybe later," I responded, "let's get that coffee you've been promising me all morning."

Peter smiled and pulled the car out of the parking lot and back towards the highway. "The Sheriff's receptionist did go to get you some. It was just your meeting was so short that she just didn't get back before we left."

In a few minutes we were back in Ruidoso. The town finally looked alive. There was considerable traffic on the main highway and a number of pedestrians on the sidewalks. The day was clear, bright and sunny. We stopped at the traffic light at the intersection just shy of the

Brown Bear Inn and the Mescalero Café. As we sat there, Peter mumbled something like "jackass". I was looking out my window at an antique store that had an old grandfather clock in the window. My parents owned one and I was always fond of them, although never had purchased one for myself.

"What's up?" I asked.

"Look at that dirt bag," he said pointing at an SUV that had obviously been extensively modified. My first guess was that it was a Ford Explorer but someone had done something to the paint job so that it took on different colors as the sunlight and shade hit it at different angles. The hubcaps also seemed to be spinning disproportionately fast for the speed the vehicle was going.

"That's Teddy Munoz. One of these days I am going to find some reason to knock him down a rung or two. His father is one of the richer guys in the county and that seems to make Little Teddy think that he can do just about anything he wants to around here."

"What's he done to the hub caps to make them spin like that?" I asked.

"Those," Peter replied smiling as though he was filling in an old man on what was happening in the real world these days, "are called spinners. A few other people in town have them. They are neat aren't they? I haven't seen another car around here with the electric paint though."

"Electric paint?" I asked.

"I'm not sure if that's the correct name for it, just what I heard Deputy Snilling call it the other day. It's rather new." Peter responded. He said all this in a way I thought he might be a bit envious of young Teddy, but I kept my thoughts to myself.

The light turned green and Deputy Blanco pulled in front of the café. As we were getting out of the car, I asked him what kind of trouble Teddy Munoz had caused for him and the town.

"A number of things, I'll tell you inside." He led me into the café and back to a table closer to the main counter. The café was still empty. In fact, not even the wait staff was in sight.

"Hey Daisy, we're back," shouted Peter. "They're probably in the back playing rummy, they are always playing rummy."

"Coming," shouted Daisy back at us as she came through a door opposite of the counter and entrance. "Oh, it's you two," she continued with a smile and a wink at me. "Couldn't find a reason to keep him in jail, Deputy?"

"Come on Daisy, you know I can't talk about the crimes and criminals in the county to just anyone," responded Peter, showing Daisy that two could play at this.

Daisy seemed to like the response. "What can I get you two?" She asked with a smile.

Peter nodded at me indicating that I should order first.

"Can I have couple of eggs over medium, some bacon and toast, and a big cup of coffee?" I asked.

"You sure may, and what about you Peter?" She asked.

"Just one of your cinnamon rolls and a cup of coffee, please."

"Sure thing," she said, "I think there is a big one back there with your name on it. Now if we can just get Kristi out here to work the counter and Larry to do the frying we may just be in business." She walked back to the door that she had come through moments ago and opened it up. "Kristi! Larry! We've got some paying customers out here, get to work."

Daisy walked over behind the counter and poured some coffee for us. The counter was fairly long with dark wood paneling all along the front facade. The top was Formica that was colored in different shades of green. The café itself was mostly light and dark browns with green table tops and window sills. Behind the counter off to one side hung the same brown bear picture that hung in my room, and likely all the other rooms at the Brown Bear Inn.

The first person that appeared in response to Daisy's summons was a man, whom I assumed was Larry. He looked about Daisy's age. He grunted at Peter as he walked by and continued on through another door that was behind the counter.

"Not much on talking is Larry," Peter remarked, "but not a bad guy. He and Daisy have been married for more years than I've been alive. They make quite a couple. She can't stop talking and he never says anything. Daisy just says that there is really no reason for him to say much, that she can do the talking for both. They have been working here for as long as I can remember. They have always been good to me and to all the folks around here. Don't believe they make much money with the café, as it is never very crowded, just enough to get by, I guess."

"Do they own the café?"

"Yes. Well, I think they do anyway," Peter qualified his answer.

"Here's your coffee. Your orders will be right out," stated Daisy as she placed the two cups and some silverware on the table. "Is it warm enough in here for you all?"

"I'm fine," I replied.

"Me, too," remarked Peter. "Daisy, did you ever meet or even see the Ribbons gal that disappeared a few days ago?"

"No, sure didn't. Heard about it. Sure is a shame. Hope she ran off with some guy and isn't out there somewhere." Her voice slowed down and softened when she said the last few words. Suddenly, putting one and one together and getting three, she looked at me and almost turned white. "Are you her Daddy?"

"No, just a friend of the family."

"Sure is a shame," she repeated, looking somewhat relieved. "Seems like we've been losing a girl a year out here for the last five or six years. They just wander off and Mother Nature doesn't give them back until spring thaw. People got too much freedom these days. My mother never would have let me take off on my own like these girls today do."

"Well, Daisy, we've had a couple guys go missing a couple of years ago, too. Remember those two cross country skiers?" Peter asked.

"Sure, I do. That was a sad one, too." Daisy looked at me and asked, "Pardon my prying, Mister but what does her family expect you to be able to do for them?"

"My name is Jim, Jim West. Between the three of us, I wish they had never called me. I have known the family for years, I knew Melissa when she was just a toddler. I think just what everyone else thinks down here, that she got herself disoriented somehow and took off in the wrong direction. Before she knew it she was lost in the night. The longer she wondered around, the more lost she became. Then it was only a matter of time." Daisy and Deputy Blanco just kept looking at me. I gathered I had not answered the question. "The family wants me to make sure every step has been taken to find their daughter. That is all. They will be arriving themselves in a couple of days. I think they just want a friend here when they show up. They are in denial, but I got the impression when I talked to them yesterday that reality was trying to break through that barrier."

"Say Deputy," Daisy remarked. "You know who did have some contact with that girl?" She didn't wait for an answer. "Marge, down at the Antler Boutique. She said the girl had come in to the Antler the day she disappeared to purchase a sweatshirt. I doubt if Marge can be of any help to your case, but you may want to talk to her. She was in here yesterday morning to have some coffee and mentioned it to Kristi and me."

Larry walked up behind Daisy and gave her a friendly nudge with the tray he was carrying. As she turned he asked her to give "the good customers" our food and asked her if Kristi had come out yet. Something in the way he said it caught Daisy's attention. She placed our breakfast in front of us, excused herself and went back through the door to the "rummy" room.

"Wonder what that was all about?" Peter commented to me.

Larry, who had just moved over to the counter, heard Peter. "Kristi's Dad has been in critical condition for a couple of days. She received a call from her Mom just as you arrived this morning. Daisy knew Kristi received a call but had come out here to take care of you two. I stayed in there with Kristi long enough to know the news was not good. Didn't sound like he was improving."

After relaying that news, Larry got up and went back into the kitchen.

"Too bad, Kristi is really a nice lady. Only been here a couple of years, I think, but really nice." After saying this,

Peter focused his attention on the giant cinnamon roll on his plate.

I turned my attention onto my own breakfast. It was very good, but I kept eyeing the cinnamon roll with envy. It didn't do any good as Peter ate the whole thing without offering to share even a small bite.

We sat there and ate our breakfast mostly in silence. Of course eating it didn't take long. When he finished the cinnamon roll, Peter asked me if I wanted to go with him to the Antler Boutique. It was nice of him to offer. We both knew it would probably be another dead end, but still he had no obligation to ask me along. I told him I would be happy to tag along.

Larry wandered back over and filled up our coffee cups as I asked for the bill.

As Larry went back to find it, Peter commented, "We could just leave it on the Sheriff's tab."

"That's all right," I said, "the two of us didn't really hit it off too well this morning, as you know. Let me take care of this."

Peter didn't put up any additional resistance. I paid the bill and the two of us left before Daisy or Kristi came out of the back room.

Chapter 4

"Wait till you meet Marge," Peter said with a smile as we got back into his car. "She is a character. Been married at least three times. Single again now, so watch out. You look like you may be her type."

Although I knew I was being set up, I had to ask. "What's her type?"

"Male, with a heart that is still beating," he said, chuckling to himself.

It was only about a three minute drive to the Antler Boutique. We drove there in silence. I was happy that it appeared my relationship with the Lincoln County Sheriff's office was going to work out okay. Deputy Blanco was a nice kid. Ideally, my work in the county would be over by the time the Sheriff came back from his trip.

Ruidoso is a pleasant, small city that makes a healthy portion of its income from the tourist trade. Consequently, there are a number of small businesses that survive on that tourist trade. The Antler boutique looked like one such place. It had a colorful blue exterior and its windows were filled with sales ads. A stranger in town walking by or even driving by could hardly miss it.

Peter parked out front, right under a big No Parking sign and we walked into the store.

"Marge here?" He asked a male clerk standing behind the cash register strategically placed by the front exit.

"Sure," the man replied, "Marge!" He shouted towards the racks of sweatshirts and sweaters in the back corner opposite of us.

A head popped up from behind one of the racks. "Yes," answered a lady I assumed was Marge.

"You have some visitors," the clerk announced.

Marge came up to us smiling. She did have a pretty smile. "Why Deputy Blanco, I haven't seen you in a while. What can I do for you?"

"Ma'am, can we talk somewhere in private?" Peter asked.

"Sure," she replied, "come back to the office." Then as we all started to walk, she looked at me and asked Peter, "Is he with us?" Maybe I was just imagining it, but the question seemed not one of concern, but rather hopeful. Peter must have read the same thing into the question as he smiled at me as we followed Marge to the back room.

Marge looked like the type of person who was determined not to let age affect her appearance. I imagined she had five to ten years on me. She was wearing tight black jeans and a red sweater that looked stretched in the right places.

"Marge," Peter started the conversation as soon as we entered the office, "this is Jim West, he is here on behalf of the parents of Melissa Ribbons, the girl that went missing a few days ago. I've been investigating that disappearance for the Sheriff's office. This morning we were talking to Daisy, up at the Mescalero, and she mentioned that you may have had some contact with the missing girl a day or two before her disappearance. Can you tell us anything about your contact with her?"

"Sure, but there isn't really much to tell. I didn't know

who she was at the time. She came in here around noon the day she went missing or the day before, looking for a big sweatshirt. Something she could put over her pajamas to sleep in. She said that the apartment they were staying in was cold at night. I helped her pick out one and she left. I wouldn't have remembered her at all if it wasn't for what happened after she left the store."

"What was that?" I asked.

"Oh that jerk Teddy Muniz, or Munoz, and a friend were out cruising in that silly car of his. They must have seen the girl walk out of the store. They honked at her, made a U-turn right in the middle of the street here and almost pulled up onto the side walk to get her attention. One of the two yelled something vulgar at her. I was at the front cash register and saw most of what happened. I went out front and yelled at him to leave the girl alone. They just laughed and drove away. She came back to me and thanked me. She looked a little shook up, but she was okay. I asked her if she needed a ride somewhere or if I could help her. She said no, that she had some friends just down the road in another store. She walked away and that was the last I saw of her."

"Did you see any more of Teddy?" Peter asked.

"No, and while he is a jerk and a couple of the gals that hang with him I think are thieves, I don't see him doing anything violent." She spoke like she knew Teddy well, but I had a feeling Deputy Blanco wasn't listening.

"Do you know which store she may have gone to after she left here?" I asked.

"No," she shook her head, "I sure don't."

We stayed a few minutes more, acknowledging how sad it was that she was now missing. Marge wished us luck and we left the store.

"Marge didn't look that dangerous," I said with a grin to Peter as we got into his car.

"Say that now Mr. West, but she'll be calling Daisy right about now, then Rose at the hotel, my guess is about ten tonight just as you are crawling into bed, she'll be calling you." I knew he was pulling my leg, but he was enjoying himself. "My girl has a friend who used to work in that store. After Marge's third husband died, she had a dozen men start calling around to see her. Allegedly last Valentine's Day she personally received six dozen roses. Not from just one person, but six different people sent her a dozen roses. I don't mean to imply anything bad about her. I've never heard anyone say anything bad about her. I like her, but she must have some ability to put a spell over men. My guess is you're next."

"I guess if it comes to that I could do worse, she is kind of attractive, probably at least ten years older than me, but again I could do worse." I was getting tired of this line of conversation. "We never did get around to talking about this Teddy guy. Do you think he could be involved?"

"Don't know but I plan to find out. If you don't mind, let me drop you off at your hotel while I do some snooping around." He pulled up by the Brown Bear Inn as he said this.

"Can I meet with you later today? I would like to talk a little bit more about your investigation."

"Sure, in fact I gave a summary of everything I did to the city police in case something spilled over from one of their cases. I'll call ahead and tell them you have my permission to look through the file if you would like." Peter offered.

"That would be great. Where is their office?"

Peter told me how to get to the city police offices and

drove off in search of his nemesis. The station was just a couple of blocks from the hotel so it would be easy to find. I was wondering why he didn't just offer to show me his file in the trunk, but I imagined the chance to "grill" Teddy had higher priority. And unlike his interview of Marge, he didn't want me along for this one.

Chapter 5

I returned to my hotel room before heading to the Ruidoso City Police. In addition to a couple of personal needs, I wanted to call John Ribbons and let him know that I was here and all was the same. Well, I didn't really want to make the call, but I knew I needed to. I felt guilty about that portion of me that wished he hadn't even called me to ask for help. Maybe it was just that I believed, as the Sheriff did, that Melissa was likely dead by now. I knew there were always chances and hope, but I believed what he wanted of me, to find his daughter alive, was undeliverable. In a couple of days John and his wife, Martha, would be showing up here in this small New Mexican town and looking into my eyes for one last glimmer of hope. I had only faced parents on a couple of times to inform them of a loss of a child. On those occasions, I really didn't know the parents and I wasn't alone. I'd hated each of those events.

I knew this was going to be different as the Ribbons already had time to digest the situation, but they were still going to look at me and me alone for the answer they wanted to hear once they arrived. And, I knew I wasn't making it any easier on myself. Last night, just as on this call, I finished the conversation with the same comment. "Don't give up hope John, there's still a chance."

I walked back out of the hotel through the lobby. No one appeared to be working. I went back out onto the street and headed in the direction Deputy Blanco had given. It was a beautiful day and the noon sun felt warm. It was hard to believe the temperature reading that was flashing on the bank's sign next door, thirty-four degrees, as I only had on a medium weight jacket and no hat. At this altitude, however, feeling warm and cold is frequently a factor of the sun shining on you, or not, as much as the actual temperature.

I passed a real estate office advertising resort property and undeveloped land. I actually owned a lot further south by Cloudcroft but had never built anything on it. It was supposed to be an investment, but to this day many beautiful areas and wishful developments in this part of the country have never really been built out.

The City Police offices did not look anywhere near as impressive as the Sheriff's complex in Carrizozo. It was basically a small office structure that could have just as well have been a store, as it was bordered on both sides by stores that seem to have the identical size and structure. Yet I imagined the stores likely did not have the obligatory holding cells in their back offices.

I walked into the station and found it quiet and peaceful. The way they should all be, but rarely are in any big city. A uniformed officer sat behind the wood paneled counter that spanned the entire foyer, blocking anyone from going too far into the station. An old couch lined the walls on each side of the door and on both side walls were matching wooden tables and chairs. It was only a few steps to the counter so it wouldn't have been hard to fill up the waiting area.

"Can I help you?" asked the officer. He looked in his mid-thirties but was already losing his thin brown hair. His uniform shirt was neatly pressed and from what I could see of him he looked in pretty good shape. "Are you Mr. West?"

The communications network in this town was starting to impress me. "Yes, I am. Did Deputy Blanco get in touch with you?"

"Yes he did, just a few minutes ago. He said to let you read the missing girl file. He said you were here on behalf of the parents. Is that correct?"

"That's right," I replied.

"If you don't mind my asking, why aren't they out here instead of you? I mean if it was my child I would have been out here the day after she disappeared."

He had a good point. "I agree with you. I can only think they were initially in a state of denial. They probably thought she had just gone off with someone and would be calling any moment. I imagine denial turned into fear after a day or two. They will be out here in a couple of days." I let my remarks hang there for a minute.

"Sad thing, though, I would hate to be in their shoes," he said, half I think to amend for his criticism of the parents and half to just fill the void in conversation. "By the way my name is Rick." He extended his hand and I shook it. His grip was firm, but not the knuckle buster of the Sheriff's. His name tag said Morrison.

"Just call me Jim," I responded in kind.

He led me through the front desk and down the hall to a small room. "Have a seat in here and I will bring you the file. Ain't much to it, Jim," he remarked as he left me alone.

The room looked like an interview room containing nothing but an empty table with two wooden chairs on one side of it and one on the other. The walls were bare. Out of habit, I looked around for the one way mirror, but there was none. I wondered if the room was wired. I had spent twenty years in the criminal investigative and counterintelligence world of the United States Air Force and had worked jointly with dozens of allied counterpart agencies and other federal and local U.S. agencies. I couldn't help checking out the room, it was second nature.

"Here it is," he said as he entered the room and put a thin stack of papers onto the table. "Take your time looking through it. If you have any questions, you know where I'll be." With that he turned and walked back out the door.

I sat down and went through the file. While the file gave a good outline of the steps taken to find Melissa, there wasn't any substance to the report at all. No one knew anything. No one saw anything at all. Melissa had a cell phone but calls made to it since she disappeared went unanswered. The last call made by anyone on the cell phone occurred hours before she disappeared. Her two friends had not seen her with any strangers since they arrived in New Mexico. The three had come the weekend before and had skied daily at Ski Apache. They had met people on the slopes and on two occasions the three of them went to clubs in Ruidoso that catered to the college age crowd. They always returned to the apartment together.

In fact, the only time Melissa wandered off on her own was the late afternoon she disappeared. As the sun sets behind the mountains it could get dark early in Nocelo, but there was enough light that she shouldn't have had any trouble catching the shuttle bus that ran hourly to and from Ruidoso and Ski Apache. The shuttle's route includes stops at a few places in between, Nocelo being one of them. Melissa knew how to get to the bus stop as the girls had taken the shuttle to and from Ski Apache a couple of times. The bus stop was only a half mile from their apartment by way of the road and only a quarter mile if one cut through the forest adjacent to the apartments.

The bus driver remembered stopping in Nocelo around four in the afternoon on the day in question and giving a couple of people a ride into Ruidoso. However, when shown a picture of Melissa, he was not sure if she was one of them. In fact, the two, possibly three people that he remembered getting on the bus were never identified in the report.

Melissa had gone to town to purchase some "feminine items" at a drug store. The report did not elaborate on what these feminine items were and I guessed it wasn't really important. No one at the drug store, a Walgreen's, could say whether she ever arrived at the store or not. Security cameras at the store provided a lot of footage of young women in dark jackets and stocking caps purchasing things throughout the evening, but none were believed to be Melissa. The report stated that the quality of the film from the old security cameras was not good, but both of Melissa's friends had reviewed the film with the police and did not believe Melissa was among of the women filmed in the store.

The bus driver was positive on the two subsequent trips back to Ski Apache that he did not drop anyone off at the Nocelo bus stop.

Deputy Blanco had interviewed a number of other residents and guests staying in the apartments and had not come up with any leads. It was as though Melissa just disappeared off the face of the earth.

While the actual report did not appear to be useful, one thing that did catch my eye was a local newspaper story on the disappearance that had been inserted in the folder that held the report. I could not tell if the page from the paper was part of the report sent over by Deputy Blanco or something placed there by the City Police. The article didn't have any new information about Melissa's disappearance - but what instantly made the hair on the back of my neck stand up were the pictures included at the end of the article that were of the people who had disappeared in the local area in the last few years, just to be discovered in the spring thaw. If you ignored the two young men, the five young women and Melissa could have all been related.

Despite the poor quality of the newspaper photos, I could easily see that each of the five young women was roughly the same age and size as Melissa, seemed to have the same hair coloring, and very familiar facial structures. What further bothered me was the sequence of their disappearances. The first was seven years ago, but the next four occurred annually going back four years from the present. Melissa, if the worst came true, would be the fifth in as many years.

I had worked enough investigations and had supervised or reviewed more than enough to be suspicious of coincidences like the one that was staring me in the face. The pattern and circumstances of these girls' deaths was too precise to be random. But why had no one else figured this out? If one girl a week had turned up missing everyone in town would be screaming about a serial killer. If one girl a month was found dead with these similarities surely someone would be suspicious. I couldn't believe just because the deaths were one year apart no one could connect the dots. Either I wasn't being told everything the police agencies were doing on the case or the skill level here in Lincoln County was way below the national average. Either way I intended to find out.

"Officer Morrison!" I called from the room. "Could you

come back here for a minute?"

"Sure," a voice replied from the front of the building. A few seconds later, he strolled in. "What can I do for you?"

"Rick," I said, trying not to be condescending, "Has anyone noticed the similarities among all these young ladies?" I looked at him for an answer, but he didn't respond right away. "They could all be sisters, couldn't they?"

"No, they aren't related," he said quickly without really getting the meaning of my question. Then some light went on somewhere in his mind, "They do look alike though, don't they? I think you have a point there. Think that could mean something?"

"I don't know." I replied, trying to be patient. "Did you ever get involved in these cases?"

"Only in a support role, Sheriff's office had lead jurisdiction in these. When I drove patrol for the city we would post pictures of the missing girls and do whatever leads we could for the Sheriff's office but we never controlled the cases. To be honest with you, until this year when I made Sergeant and took over the running of the office for Captain Jones, I had never even seen a report on any of the missing girls. Never thought it was my job to second guess the Sheriff."

I wasn't sure if his final remark was meant to take any criticism off himself, or if he was giving me an oblique word of advice not to second guess the Sheriff.

"I wouldn't expect you to," I responded. "Do you have copies of the prior cases here?"

"We may have last years, but as we weren't lead on any of the investigations, we would have only kept the other reports a year after they were closed. Then we shred them.

But, the Sheriff's office would still have them."

"Could you see if you can find the file on last year's incident?" I asked.

Fortunately he didn't challenge my need or authority to see it. Perhaps I had kindled his curiosity and he too wanted to see what it contained. He was only gone a few minutes and returned with a small file in hand.

"As you can see there really isn't much in this file," he said in a discouraged tone. "Just the missing girl report, a chronological list of steps taken without any elaboration and the coroner's report. Feel free to go through it. I don't think anyone would care."

He handed me the file. Rather than leave this time, he sat in the chair opposite me and picked up the newspaper article on Melissa's disappearance and started reading it. I wondered if he had read it before. Odd if he hadn't I thought, but it didn't really seem to matter so I turned my attention to last year's file.

Sergeant Morrison was correct. There was very little detail in the report. Penny James had been a twenty two year old grad student vacationing in Ruidoso over the holidays with her husband Sean. They were from El Paso, Texas. On their third day in Ruidoso, Sean left Penny in town while he went skiing alone at Ski Apache. Penny had gone skiing with him the first two days but wanted to shop and sightsee and used the excuse that she was sore to stay behind. When Sean returned to the hotel Penny was gone. He had contacted the authorities later that night. The search began. With Sean's consent the police even went through the hotel room looking for any signs of a struggle. There was none. The normal bulletins and other regular administrative steps for a missing person case had been done. Nothing occurred until late March of this year when a hiker found her body.

Since the body was found outside Ruidoso in the county, the Sheriff's office took the lead in the case. But the investigation was never really re-opened. The county coroner simply issued his report. Penny had died from a combination of a fall and exposure. She was found among some large boulders at the base of a fairly steep ridgeline. The theory set forth was that she was either jogging or hiking along the dirt trail that ran along the top of the ridgeline and somehow had fallen off the side. The examination of the body indicated that the fall had not killed Penny but rather had rendered her seriously injured and likely unconscious. The cold weather killed her. The snow drifts are unusually high in the ravine where she was found due to the normal wind patterns in the area.

The report did not include any indication that anything else was done to resolve the disappearance and death.

I looked up at Morrison, "Do you remember anything about Penny's body being found or what happened afterwards?"

"Other than what was in the newspaper, I really don't. She was found outside our jurisdiction and everyone said it appeared to be an accident. I know you are thinking there might be some connection to this year's missing girl but I don't remember in any of the past incidents or even this one, that there has ever been a shred of evidence indicating that each was anything but an accident." Morrison paused. "If there is a connection, that would mean we have someone who is targeting young blonds, just to kidnap them and throw them down mountains. That seems somewhat far-fetched."

I smiled in acknowledgement, "I know.   I am just reaching at straws hoping Melissa might still be alive. But it's worth the effort and I have the time. Thanks a lot for your help Rick." I stood up to leave and he guided me back out to the lobby.

"Let me know if I can do anything for you, Jim. I mean it and good luck." He said as I left the building. I appreciated his offer.

Chapter 6

I walked back towards the hotel. The temperature at the bank was flashing forty degrees. It felt warmer in the sun. The same sign was also flashing one o'clock. I wasn't very hungry but a bowl of chili might get me through the rest of the afternoon. I also thought the staff at the Mescalero Café might be able to answer a couple of questions for me.

A group of five or six ladies walked out of the café as I approached the door. They were all laughing and shouting their goodbyes to Daisy as they exited. I held the door for the last of the group to leave, but none of them seemed to notice me as they walked out and away. There is something to be said about being nondescript, but around groups of the opposite sex that normally isn't one's goal. Shoving the fleeting disappointment aside, as I didn't want to dwell on the fact that it had been a while since I was young and in great shape, I entered the café.

Daisy was walking back towards the long counter and another lady was cleaning off the recently vacated table. Her back was to me but I guessed she was Kristi. Two elderly gentlemen occupied the table I had taken that morning. The rest of the tables were empty. I selected a table near the counter.

Daisy noticed me first and smiled. "Well, welcome back Mr. West. How did your visit with Marge go?"

"Fine, although she had nothing new to add. And please

call me Jim."

"Sure, Jim, are you here for lunch?"

"Yes, I am. Could I see a menu?"

Her response was to look at the other waitress and confirm my hunch. "Kristi, give Mr. West, I mean Jim, here a menu." And then back to me, "I need a break, but Kristi will take good care of you." She walked through the door that led to the kitchen.

"Here you go," came a voice beside me.

I glanced up, taking the menu from her. She was an impressive lady. That may not be the best way to describe her but I was impressed. She had dark brown hair and a face that kind of reminded me of Audrey Hepburn.

"Can I get you a drink?" She asked as I quickly perused the menu.

"Just water please, with a big bowl of chili. That's all I'll be having for lunch." I watched her as she walked away. Just average height and build, but she had a nice walk.

She was only gone a minute or two before she returned with a bowl of steaming chili, crackers and a large glass of ice water. The bowl was a big bowl.

"Here you go," she said again. "Enjoy your lunch." She turned to walk away.

"Thanks," I said. She turned and nodded. She looked preoccupied and I remembered her phone call that morning. I hoped all was well with her father.

I ate the chili in silence. It was good. They had sprinkled some shredded cheddar cheese on top of it and onions had been cooked into the chili. As I ate I tried to prioritize the next steps to take. While the odds were still great that Melissa's disappearance had been an accident, there was at least now a course of action to take. Go with the hypothesis that the disappearances are connected and find the links. There were some obvious ones. All girls – forget the boys. All of similar age and appearance. All disappearing in a ten mile radius and found in a much smaller radius. More info was needed. I would need to get with Deputy Blanco and dissect the prior cases to determine if there are any additional similarities.

"How's the chili?" Kristi had walked back into the room and approached my table.

"Very good," I replied honestly.

"There's more in the kitchen if you are still hungry," she said. After I told her I'd be lucky to finish the big bowl she brought me, she stayed. "Daisy said you are here looking for the missing girl from Florida. I wish you luck. It's such a sad thing."

"Did you ever meet Melissa?" I asked.

"No, I don't believe so. We don't get large crowds in here but enough tourists come and go that I could never be sure who may have been here once."

"Are you familiar with the past disappearances that have occurred here in the Ruidoso area? The other girls that have gone missing only to be found in the spring?"

"Not really," she responded, "I mean, I know it seems to happen almost every year or so, but other than feel sorry for the victims and their families I never paid much attention to the actual incidents. I've had enough sad things happen in my life; I don't dwell on others' misfortunes."

I wish I could have said the same, but in my life, or at least my professional career, I had spent too much time focused on the negative events in the lives of others.

"Do you have any idea what may have happened to the girl?" she asked.

"No, not yet. I'm not too optimistic either, but let's not get ourselves too depressed, there still are a few things to be checked out and eliminated." I knew I was stretching it a little, but for some reason I felt a need to not make Kristi's day any more negative than it probably already was. "How long have you lived here in Ruidoso?" I asked changing the subject.

"Don't I look like a native?" She challenged me with a trace of a smile. "I'm from Lubbock, Texas, originally. Been here about four years. I came here to escape a bad experience. Got here on the bus on a Saturday morning with about twenty dollars in my purse. I really didn't know what I was going to do, but the good Lord apparently had it all planned out. We are just a couple of blocks from the station and while walking down the road out front, I saw a sign in the window of this café advertising for a waitress. I walked in and have been here ever since. Daisy and her family have been very good to me." She paused for a second, "Sorry, I didn't mean to tell you my whole life story."

I told her that it was okay, that I had some time to kill - which wasn't true.

She went to get the water pitcher to refill my water glass. The other two customers in the café got up and left.

When she returned with the water, I asked her if her family was still in Lubbock.

"I spent the first twenty five years of my life in Lubbock," she began. I liked her voice. "My childhood was pretty much normal. I enjoyed school. I was even a girl scout for a couple of years. I took a shot at college at Texas Tech but fell in with the wrong crowd. I refer to my college years as my rebel years. I ended up with a group of students who partied and protested more that we studied. By the end of my freshman year my grades were lousy. I think I only passed one class. As you can imagine my parents weren't too thrilled and responded by cutting off my financial support. I don't blame them at all. I dropped out of school and started working for an advertising firm. The job was interesting and I began to get my life back in order. I even contemplated going back to college, but then Stan came along." She paused here and asked, "Am I boring you?"

"No, not at all," I responded. "Why don't you have a seat for a few minutes?"

She did. Something was definitely troubling her and for whatever reason she wanted someone to talk to, and it looked as though that person was going to me. On most occasions I would have found this annoying, but not today. At the time I didn't know why but looking back I should have guessed why I didn't feel annoyed.

Kristi related that shortly after starting work, Stanley G. Parkins was hired into the same advertising firm as its new Vice President for Marketing. He was nearly ten years older than Kristi but they hit it off from the start. She began dating him shortly after his arrival and they were married within a year. Her parents weren't very happy as they thought he was too old for her, but as he seemed to be a good "catch" in every other way their protests were short lived.

For a while everything was great. The first incident, as she referred to them, didn't occur for several months. They had an argument. Kristi couldn't even remember what it was about, but it had ended with Stanley hitting her with his fist. The blow was so hard it knocked her to the ground and dazed her. She thought he had broken her jaw but he hadn't.

"I should have left him that day," Kristi stated, "but I

didn't. I'm not even sure any more why I didn't. Stan immediately apologized to me and I secluded myself for days until the bruising and swelling went down."

Again Kristi paused for a moment before going on. I remained silent. She continued explaining that nothing else happened for almost a year. Then, one day at work, Stanley got into an argument that turned into a shoving match with another company VP. It would have likely turned into a full-fledged fight if others in the office hadn't physically pulled the two apart. Unfortunately for Stanley he ended the confrontation with a string of old fashioned cuss words criticizing the VP and the rest of the management of the company. The next morning Stanley was fired. He came home spoiling for a fight and vented his rage on Kristi. Initially just yelling at her for a variety of things, he soon became violent and beat her unconscious. When she came to he was out of the house. Without a second thought she grabbed whatever was essential and left him.

Her flight to safety took her home. She thought she would be safe with her parents. Her folks immediately took her to the hospital and along with a nurse at the hospital, convinced her to make a report of what happened to the police. He had knocked out a tooth and her face was so swollen that it didn't take much convincing to get the police to go looking for him.

However, when they got back to her parents' house that evening Stanley was waiting for them.

"We didn't see him at first. He was waiting, probably hiding, by an old oak in our side yard. Once we got out of my dad's car he attacked us."

"Attacked you?" I asked. "What do you mean?"

"Just what I said - he ran over and grabbed me,

screaming incoherently! My dad grabbed him and the next thing we were all in a big fight, right there in the front yard. Mom and I didn't do much but distract him a little and got bruised up for our effort. Can you believe he actually hit my Mom?" I nodded to acknowledge I could believe it. "But I think our being there gave my dad enough help to hold his own. At the time I was terrified, I think we all were. Looking back I am so proud of my dad. You know he is a lot older than Stanley."

"Well, what happened?" I was hooked at this point and certainly wanted to know how it all ended.

"All the commotion caused the neighbors to come out. Someone called the police and two or three of the men came over and ended up holding Stanley down until the police arrived."

"Hope he ended up in jail. That's where he belonged."

"That's the good part. He did. He got into a shoving match with one of the policemen when they tried to put the cuffs on him. They sprayed him with pepper spray, or something like that, cuffed him anyway and took him to jail. We got a restraining order which did keep him away. He ended up pleading guilty and got eight months in jail."

"I'm glad he did, but I'm also surprised he went to jail. Usually guys like that get off on probation right away." I've known too many situations where the jerks never spent any real time behind bars.

"They told me that he spent time in jail because of the assault when he came after my whole family. I guess that made it more serious than just attacking me. The resisting arrest charge they tagged on also didn't help him any either." She grinned as she made the last remark.

"Once he was in jail, I came down here. Only my parents

know where I am. Everyone else writes to me at my parents and they forward the mail to me or they just use e-mail. My parents know to call me at the restaurant and anyone can call me on my cell. It still has a Lubbock area code."

"That's smart," I said to reassure her.

As if she was reading my thoughts, she started talking again. "I know he can probably find me if he tries hard enough, my hope is that I made it just too much of an effort for him and he'll never really try. Every now and then I see someone coming into the restaurant or walking down the street, who, for just a second, I think is Stanley. He still scares me. I never, never want to see him again. I guess I'll just have to live with that fear for the rest of my life."

"Do you know if has made any attempt to contact or find you since he was released from prison?" I asked.

"Right after he was released, he called my folks and asked for me. They told him I had moved to Europe. They then called the police, and the police, I was told, personally talked to him and reminded Stanley that he was not to make any further attempts to contact me." She rolled her eyes at this as though to indicate she didn't know if the police caution would have much of an effect on him. "He never contacted my parents again, but a couple of times he ran into old friends of mine and asked them if they had an address for me. Nothing lately, though, so maybe he has moved on. I hope so."

"I imagine he has," I said, mainly to try to reassure her.

"Sorry I made you listen to my boring life story. Your turn, tell me more about yourself. Is Jim short for James?" She smiled.

"No, just Jim, never been a James."

I liked this lady. She was attractive and I felt sorry for

her. But, the last thing I wanted to do was talk about me. In fact, I rarely like talking about myself.

"Not much to say, I spent twenty years in the Air Force and retired a few years back. I do a few things here and there to stay busy."

"Like this trip to Ruidoso for your friend?" She interrupted.

"Yes, on occasion. But this is not typical. I'm not a private investigator. I just seem to get roped into these projects sometimes, but this is not what I do normally. I get a pension from the Air Force which allows me to do some part time guest lecturing at colleges and to civic organizations rather than work full time. I like to be in control of my calendar. It's a luxury I didn't use to have. Not being married has helped in that regard too."

Maybe it was the way I said it that caused her to ask, "Were you married?" Perhaps it was just innocent curiosity.

"I was once, for a number of years, in the end it just didn't work out." This was definitely not a subject I wanted to get into. Time to shift the topic I thought. "Have you noticed, or has anyone ever discussed with you, the similarities of the girls that went missing each winter here over the last four or five years? Each girl was then found during the spring thaw."

"No, not at all. Other than each being a tragic thing to have happened, I don't remember any conversation about similarities. What makes you ask that?"

I didn't expect to her to have much to say and was just content that I was no longer the topic of conversation. "I asked because when I looked at the pictures of each of the young ladies, I was amazed at how similar they all looked. If you didn't know better they could have all been related.

Each girl was a blond, about five and a half feet tall, average build, none too skinny, none too fat, and all were around twenty years old."

Kristi responded to my summary with growing interest. "That is a bit unusual. I would have thought that a brunette or a red head would have been among the mix. I would have also expected different sizes. You know, even within families you get different sizes and shapes. I have three cousins in my Dad's brother's family who have similar coloring to their hair and complexion but one is tall and somewhat thin and the other two are normal height but one is real stocky. And that's being polite. But even if these girls look alike, other than being a coincidence, what do you think that means?"

"I don't know, but there is no doubt if each one of these girls went missing in five consecutive weeks, everyone would be looking at this disappearance entirely different. If that were the case, it would look like someone was specifically targeting young gals that fit that description and only that description." I was talking to Kristi, but I was also again trying to get my head around this conundrum of divergent probabilities. When taken individually it was most probable each disappeared and died as previously concluded by the authorities in their respective investigations. However, when looked at as a whole the odds were moving rapidly away from the incidents being unrelated and accidental.

"I see what you mean, but it seems like a big stretch to think that we have some crazy guy sacrificing young blond virgins by throwing them off mountain tops during the winter solstice." She responded, somewhat sarcastically.

"I know, but stranger things have happened in this world

of ours. I'm not saying that all these incidents were not just tragic accidents. In fact, up to a few hours ago, I was fairly confident that Melissa's disappearance was just what everyone has concluded, another accident. Now though, there are too many alarms going off in my brain to accept all these as coincidence."

"So what are you going to do?" She asked.

"Try to convince the Sheriff's office to reopen their cases on all the victims but I don't think they will." I didn't want to tell Kristi that I was going to have to dig deeper on my own, perhaps even get into a little head butting with the sheriff's office. On the positive side, for the first time since getting the original call, I had some hope that Melissa could still be alive. While that was a little reassuring, if she was alive it also significantly increased the pressure on me to find her before it was too late. I had no idea who was kidnapping these young girls or how long they were keeping them alive. However I did know that if there was a kidnapper, he was also a killer and the clock that had Melissa's name on it was likely running out of time.

I ended up spending an hour talking to Kristi. It wasn't intentional, on my part or hers. Looking back, I believe she just needed someone to talk to that afternoon. Maybe I did too.

Chapter 7

The restaurant had been without customers for a while, so when the door opened from the outside I turned to see Sergeant Rick Morrison of the Ruidoso city police enter the restaurant in an agitated state.

"Mr. West, you'd better come with me." He instructed rather than asked.

"Sure," I responded. "What's up, did you find Melissa?"

"No." Then looking at Kristi but talking to me, "how long have you been here?"

"I came straight from your office, about one o'clock."

"That's right Rick. After he finished eating, Mr. West and I have just been sitting here talking."

"What's up?" I asked again.

Morrison looked at both of us for a second, apparently finally deciding that it would be all right to talk to us. "Detective Blanco's police car was found in a ditch about two miles south of town. It looks like someone pushed it into the ditch. The brake was off and the car was in neutral. Blanco's missing and he isn't answering his radio or phone. The Sheriff's office has an APB out on you. The instructions are to pick you up, with force if necessary, as you were the last person seen with him and supposedly still with him."

"He dropped me off and I went straight to your office. From there I came here. Peter was heading out to talk to some Munoz or Muniz character. I don't think he wanted me along. That's who you should be looking for, not me."

"I figured you had nothing to do with his disappearance. You showed up at the headquarters within minutes of his call to me about you. It didn't make sense to me, that's why I came looking for you. I called your hotel and Rose said she thought she saw you come over here for lunch. I thought I better find you before some of the Sheriff's deputies did."

"Well I guess I'm all yours, Sergeant Morrison, but I am not sure what help I can be to you."

"I just think it would be better if I physically took you to them and was there when they talked to you. If they are predisposed to thinking you had something to do with his disappearance they may not act very professional. You don't need that and I don't like that. Too many hot heads in the Sheriff's office if you ask me." He shook his head slightly as if to emphasize this last statement.

"Well I appreciate that Rick." I hoped using his first name wouldn't put him off as I did appreciate his consideration. "I guess I'm ready to go when you are."

We both excused ourselves from Kristi and walked out of the restaurant.

He pointed to his police vehicle parked close to the restaurant. "Let's drive out to the location where they found Blanco's car. I think there will still be some deputies there. Hopefully we will be able to clarify everything there and remove you from their sights."

Good idea, I thought and jumped into the cruiser. It was a fairly new Chrysler sedan, souped up a little for the police, no doubt. "Are they in your jurisdiction?" I asked.

"No, it's just outside city limits. But they won't mind our being out there. I don't think they are treating it as an active crime scene, at least not yet." He stepped on the gas and we shot out of the parking spot.

"Good pick up," I said referring to the acceleration.

"They are fast." Morrison agreed with a grin. "We've chased down a few guys with these new cars. The department got three of them last year. I like them."

We drove out of the city and within a couple of minutes turned off the main road onto a narrow road that seemed to be barely paved. It ran perpendicular to the main road and quickly ran over a small rise. As it did I had a good view of Ruidoso sprawled out slightly below us. We were quite close to town. We traveled on another half mile then came to a stop next to two cars distinctly marked as belonging to the sheriff's department. Backed halfway down into a fairly steep ditch was a wrecker. The mechanic was in the process of hooking the wrecker's tow line to another vehicle which I assumed was the one Deputy Blanco had been driving. Four uniformed deputies were watching the mechanic from the side of the road.

As we got out of our vehicle and started walking towards the deputies, they turned and looked at us. "Hey Joe, you ought to be down there helping out. Afraid you'll get your shoes muddy?" Sergeant Morrison said with a grin.

The oldest of the four deputies, who I imagined was Joe, turned and smiled at Morrison.

"Smart ass. Are you out here to see how the professionals handle things?"

"That will be the day. Actually, Joe, I hear you guys are looking for Mr. West." He nodded towards me. "I had been with him in town so I brought him out to see what we could do for you."

At the mention of my name, the other three deputies who had been half listening to the banter turned and focused their attention on me.

"Relax boys," Sergeant Morrison injected. "He has been in town since Deputy Blanco dropped him off around noon. He was with me and then with Kristi at the Mescalero Café. I double checked times and everything. He couldn't have been involved with this."

Joe, who I took for the senior of the three deputies, walked over to me. I offered my hand but he didn't take it. He obviously was not quite ready to declare me innocent. I couldn't blame him. He had a missing deputy and I was the easiest solution they had. I was supposed to be driving around with him.

"It's true," I said. "I know nothing about this. Deputy Blanco dropped me off in town to review the file on the missing girl, Melissa Ribbons. He was heading off to try to find a guy named Munoz or Muniz. Peter and I had just learned that Munoz had been seen giving Melissa a hard time on the day of her disappearance. Nothing was said that would specifically tie Munoz to the disappearance, but there was enough that Peter wanted to go find him and talk to him without my being there. I have not seen or talked to him since he dropped me off in town."

"As I said," added Morrison, "I can verify West's presence in town."

"All right, let's say for now you are not involved in this. Once we get this car out I would still like to talk to you in private." Deputy Joe said this to me but then looked at Morrison.

"Okay, I can take a hint. If one of you will give Mr. West a lift back into town when you are done with him, I'll head back now."

Joe acknowledged the request and Morrison turned,

walked back to his car and after doing a nice tight u-turn headed towards town.

The tow truck began winching in the car, lifting the rear of the car up and towards the back of the wrecker. Everyone turned to watch. Keeping his eyes on the car and not looking at me, Joe started talking.

"West, the Sheriff asked me to keep an eye on you. He said you had a habit of causing trouble and sticking your nose in where it doesn't belong. I don't know what all trouble you have caused in the past but I sure hope you don't plan on causing any while you're here. I like Sergeant Morrison and if he took the time to come out here with you then I'll cut you some slack but I don't need the Sheriff on my case because of you. Are you going to be in town long?"

"Just a few days," I answered.

He nodded finally looking at me.

"Joe," one of the other deputies spoke for the first time, "if Peter went looking for Teddy Munoz alone, that could be the answer to all this. There is bad blood between those two and Teddy's got a gang that is pretty loyal to him. You know we think they have been involved in a lot of the shit that goes on around here. You think maybe Zack and I should head over to the old man's house and see if they know anything?"

"Yeah, good idea, go ahead and take Luke with you. It will be a little crowded but an extra body might be a good idea. I'll take Mr. West back to town once the wrecker starts rolling."

The three deputies got into the front car and after making a u-turn drove back in the direction we had come. The wrecker pulled onto the road immediately after the deputies left. The driver leaned out the window and said something to Joe that I didn't catch and drove off in the same direction taken by everyone else.

"Well let's go," said Joe and motioned to his car.

"Thanks, my first name is Jim."

"I know," said Joe and gave me a smile which I wasn't sure meant let's be friends or don't worry I know all about you and will be happy to step on you if necessary. "I think we can go straight down this road for another half mile and catch a dirt road that will get us back into town a little quicker. These foothills have a lot of dirt roads and trails. They're mostly unmarked so you just have to remember where they are and where they go."

We drove in silence for the next minute as he found the turn off that he wanted. We turned right onto a one lane dirt road that didn't look in very good shape.

"This may not have been a very good idea," Joe murmured, half to himself.

"Where is the Munoz property?" I asked.

"The main ranch is about six miles further down the road you took out of town with Sergeant Morrison. But they own pockets of land all over this county. We're close to some of their property right now. In all they own a few thousand acres, most of it is on the main ranch." He nodded to his side of the car when he mentioned the land close by.

We had not traveled very far when Joe had to bring the car to a sudden halt. A city or county construction crew had cut a ditch through the road. A bobcat vehicle and a small tractor with a nasty looking digging apparatus poking out the front of it were parked by the side of the road. There was no one around. Both vehicles had the official county logo on the side doors. Joe grunted. "I wonder what the county is doing out here. I guess the growth of the region is constantly making them expand the water, electric or some other system."

"Well it is beautiful country. Can't blame people for coming out here."

Joe started backing the car up to find a place to turn around. "Guess we can't go that way. Sorry for the delay."

"No problem," I said as he began a slow u-turn that took us up a side of an incline. As we reached the highest point of the incline I got a look at the valley below and saw a metal building in a small clearing below. Parked next to it was Teddy's SUV.

"There's Munoz' vehicle," I remarked to Joe. "I don't see anything else."

Joe stopped the car, got out and walked around to my side. I got out too.

"Interesting," was all he said. "Let's see if we can't find a way down there and see what's going on."

From where I stood, I didn't see any way to drive down to the building. Part of me wanted to just say drop me off in town on your way there, but I was worried about Peter. I also wanted to suggest he call for some backup, but I figured he would do so once we got there. I needed to build rapport with as many of the sheriff's people as I could. I knew my anticipated meddling in his case would not be welcome.

We returned to the car and he began driving back the way we came but rather than turn left when the dirt road met the road, we turned right and away from where Peter's vehicle was found. The proximity of that location to where we were now headed raised some caution flags in my mind and I supposed in Deputy Joe's. He drove on without talking.

We had only traveled another half mile or so when Joe

again stopped the car. Right in front of us was another narrow dirt road that led off in the direction of the metal building. Although we couldn't see the building because of the thick shrubbery and scattered Pinon trees, my surmise was supported by Joe getting out of the vehicle and shoving open a small gate that blocked the entrance. A sign was hanging from the gate. On it was written "Private Property – Trespassers will be fed to the dogs."

As Joe got back in the car I commented, "Not a very neighborly sign."

"People like their humor around here. The most common one is 'Trespassers will be shot'. So far we've either had a shortage of trespassing or a more forgiving population as I don't remember a single occasion when the threats have ever been carried out."

Joe pulled onto the narrow trail, barely wide enough for one car and we proceeded slowly. We didn't close the gate behind us. "The main driveway is on the far side of the property. We would have to go back thru town and come in a different way to get to it. Luckily I remembered seeing that sign before and realized it could only lead to the building as it is on the Munoz property. They have around fifteen acres here, maybe a little more."

We had only driven a short time when we rounded a bend and got a glimpse of the building. From this side we were not able to see Teddy's car. Our view was quickly cut off again by another patch of bushes and trees. Finally we rounded the last curve and were within a dozen yards of the building. There were no markings on the building and nobody in sight.

Joe kept the car some ten yards away from the building and pulled off to the side of the little clearing most likely used as a parking area. "Looks peaceful, you can get out but stay here with the car."

"Shouldn't you call for backup?" I asked.

"I don't think anyone is here."

A rookie mistake, I thought, but didn't say anything.

We both got out of the car. I actually had a little difficulty getting out as he had pulled the car next to and behind a thick area of Pinon trees and the wild shrubbery that covers a lot of the undeveloped land in these foothills. In fact, from where we parked I couldn't even see the building.

Once I got out, I looked over the roof of the car at him. He was staring at the building. Probably having second thoughts about calling for that backup I thought. The sun was starting to get low and the shadows were casting an ominous darkness over more and more of the land surrounding us. However, he just looked at me and whispered "Stay here."

We closed our doors in unison and he turned and walked away. I studied the ground and bushes adjacent to my side of the car. I noticed something that looked like a piece of clothing on the ground about five yards into the underbrush. I decided that was probably within my authorized area to roam so I went to investigate. It was nothing but a rag. As I was crouching over the rag looking at it, I heard the sounds of a short struggle and a thump, then a second one. The hairs on the back of my neck shot up immediately. I recognized that sound.

"Hey Pico, that's enough. You'll kill him." I heard a voice say.

"Who cares, he's a cop. They should all be killed," said a second voice. The second voice then continued, "I thought I saw another person in the car when it rounded the corner."

"Pico, you are seeing things. I only saw him. Go take a look if you want. I'm going in to see what Teddy wants done with this guy.   Go look, this cop's not going anywhere."

"Julio, don't you want to come with me?"

"Okay, okay, let's go look."

I crouched down even further and moved into an area where I thought the underbrush was a little thicker. I didn't think they would see me from the car but they wouldn't have to come in very deep to find me.

I could see movement by the car and every now and then a clear glimpse of one or the other of the two men. They were both in their early twenties, wearing leather jackets, one fairly short and other medium height. Both had Latino or Mexican features, but that was common throughout New Mexico. They had been speaking English.

"See, Pico, no one is here. Let me go talk to Teddy and you watch the cop. He isn't going anywhere but we might as well keep an eye on him."

"I want his gun."

"It's okay with me, man, but let me talk to Teddy."

They both walked away.

Chapter 8

I stayed still for a few minutes. My situation was not good. I was unarmed. I did not have keys to any car within a couple of miles. If I wanted to flee, I really didn't even know which way to go. It was getting late in the day and I wasn't wearing a heavy coat. Besides that there were at least three people here that were armed with at least one gun now, likely more. On the positive side, it was Joe lying there on the cold ground with his head bashed in, not me.

I backed slowly away and checked my cell phone to ensure it was on silent and to see if I had a signal. I did not. The small valley we were in was surrounded by hills.

I was tempted to go back to the sheriff's car in the off chance Joe left his keys there. I was pretty sure he hadn't, but I was thinking there might be something useful there, like the radio and maybe a shotgun or something. Unfortunately, by the time I decided to make my move Julio showed back up with a third individual. After some brief comments that I couldn't quite hear, Julio and Pico started dragging Joe towards the car and the third individual disappeared. A few seconds later I heard the rumble of a diesel engine and the sound of a vehicle moving in the direction of the sheriff's vehicle. It was a big Ford pickup and it pulled adjacent to the others just as they were putting Joe into the back seat of his car.

"Follow me out and stay close. Teddy wants us all back

by six," said the driver in the pickup.

The pickup moved slowly up the dirt road away from the building. It just took a few seconds for the other two to follow. I didn't know who was driving. I felt bad about what was going to happen to Joe. I didn't think they were just going to abandon him, but the odds did not favor my unarmed frontal assault against three likely armed men. Unfortunately, I knew that I had to do something and something fast. Three of the opposition had just driven off. I had to use that to my favor.

I looked around and saw no one else outside but neither had Joe and I earlier. There wasn't a door or a window on the side of the building that I faced. The building itself looked like a small warehouse or garage facility, about forty yards in length and tall enough to be two stories. I moved quickly, paralleling my side of the building and trying to stay in some cover. It only took a few seconds to be adjacent to the corner. I moved on, rounding the corner. The underbrush was thinner, but I still saw no one. There was a jeep parked on this side but nothing else. The building had a door and three windows. This side was also narrower, maybe twenty five yards in width. The door was in the center of the wall and two of the windows sat on opposite sides of the door, probably for offices. The third window was a larger one and was higher up above the window on the right side of the door. There was light coming from the lower right window but the other two were dark. All appeared to have curtains that were closed.

I went as far as the next corner. No doors or windows but there was a paved parking lot. Teddy's Ford Explorer was still there. A driveway led back up a hill and disappeared quickly in the brush. There was a lot of open space to traverse but I needed to look at the last side of the building. I needed to see if there was another way in and out. I thought there would be. More importantly I wanted to ensure there weren't a lot of motorcycles or cars parked there. That would be really, really bad.

I ran to the end of the building. There was no indication that anyone saw me. Finally, lady luck was on my side. No motorcycles, cars, not even a bicycle was parked there. The wall on this final side had three large garage type doors. The closest of them was open about a foot or two off the ground, probably for some ventilation.

I moved quickly out of the meager cover I had and towards the open garage door. Dropping to the ground, I peered inside. Although it was dark inside, I could make out the outlines of a tractor and two large flatbed trailers. The ceiling looked too high for another level above the garage. No one seemed to be inside.

Staying as low to the ground as I possibly could, I squeezed under the door and into the large one room garage. Once inside, my eyes adjusted quickly. The sides of the rooms were lined with various tools, work tables and cans of what looked like both paint and oil. I grabbed a wrench. "Better than nothing," I mumbled to myself. There was no ceiling to the garage other than the roof. Despite the high roof and the cold outside, it was comfortable inside the garage. More than it should have been, I thought. I could see two doors leading from the garage to the rest of the building. I tried the first one and it was locked. I listened at the door and heard nothing. I went to the second. I listened first, this time, and could hear voices and laughter. It was unlocked.

I opened the door slowly. Besides the light which I expected, the first thing I noticed was the heat. For whatever reason, this part of the building was being kept very warm.

I stepped inside and closed the door behind me. I stood still and surveyed my situation. I was in a short hallway. The ceiling here indicated there may be a second story. Two rooms opened off the hallway about ten feet in front of me. The one on the left looked dark and unoccupied. The one on the right was lit and I could now hear the humming or soft singing coming from someone, likely female, in that room. The door to that room was partially closed. The door at the end of the hallway was also open an inch or two. Male voices, two I guessed, were coming from somewhere beyond that door. The floor was covered with an indoor-outdoor carpet that originally was probably grey but was now spotted with grease, oil, and mud stains.

I moved quietly down the hall and peered into the room that I believed was occupied by the singing lady. It was a kitchen and the lady had her back to the door doing something on the counter. I was considering slipping past the door and proceeding down the hall to check out the next area when my luck dried up. The lady turned and looked right at me. She was young, probably early twenties, and like the other three appeared to be of Mexican descent. She wasn't dressed for winter, wearing just jeans, sandals and a t-shirt. Tight, no bra, I tried not to notice.

"Who are you?" She asked, none too friendly. I realized she had a sharp kitchen knife in her hand. She had been cutting some sausage at the counter. The knife was now pointed at me. Not yet in a threatening way, more in a way to say 'Hey, do you happen to see this big knife in my hand, Mister?' I saw it.

"Teddy said I could come back here -" she didn't let me finish.

She tilted her head towards the direction of the male voices and started to shout for Teddy. I don't think she got to the second d in the name before I slugged her hard hitting her on the temple and sending her into a nice sleep that I hoped would last long enough for me to do what I had to do here and get out. She collapsed into my arms and I laid her gently on the floor. I now had a knife and a wrench in my arsenal. Things were picking up.

I know it's impolite to hit women and I rarely do. But this was one of those times when there was no option. This group of people were not the kind with whom you take chances, not after what they did to Deputy Joe and probably Peter. I had no illusions that they would just want to give me a lift back to town.

I looked around for a phone. I didn't see one in the room. I left the room intending to check the room across the hall. As I entered the hall, however, I heard a voice yell, "You are crazy man! You will never get away with this!"

The voice was Peter's and it came from somewhere past the end of the hallway. He sounded furious and afraid, but he was obviously still alive. I moved quickly to the end of the hallway and looked through the small opening of the door. I had to open the door a little further to get a glimpse inside.

I could see one person sitting on a chair, probably Teddy. There were two other chairs next to his but they were unoccupied. He was looking into a concrete pit built into the floor. My first impression was that the pit was similar to those you see at the places you get your oil changed. Teddy was looking into the pit and laughing. From my angle, I couldn't see anything in the pit. He had a bowl of something in his lap. As I was watching, he reached into the bowl and threw what looked like a small rock into the pit. As soon as it hit the floor of the pit I heard a sound that made me involuntarily take a small step backwards. It was the loud rattle of a rattlesnake, followed by a second rattlesnake.

"I'm going to kill you when I get out of here!" Peter shouted.

Teddy just laughed and reached into the bowl again. "You're tiring out fool! I bet those snakes get you in the next five minutes. You'll never get out of there."

Suddenly a form appeared right on the other side of the door. It was the second male I had heard talking. He pushed the door open and into me, knocking me backwards. He was as startled to see me as I was to see him.

His reaction was a lot faster than the young lady now napping in the kitchen. He immediately lunged at me. I swung the wrench at him and caught him on the side of the head. Unfortunately my backward momentum took some power out of the blow. He grimaced but still managed to grab both my arms with his hands. He had a strong grip and we danced awkwardly in the small hallway. I tried to knee him in the crotch but just hit his leg. He smashed his head into mine. It hurt but not enough to slow me down. I head butted him back and luckily split his eyebrow. Blood started streaming into his left eye. Advantage me. There wasn't enough room in the hallway for either of us to get much leverage. He was determined not to let go of my arms and I was doing my best to hang onto my weapons and use them.

We were probably only ten or fifteen seconds into the fight when we rolled out of the hallway into the outer area where Teddy was sitting. As we rolled around I broke free. He was on his back and I was on my knees next to him. He lashed out with his right leg, hitting me in the elbow. I dropped the wrench but countered by slashing out with the knife in my left hand and sliced him deep in his right side. He reacted by coiling himself to his right to protect the knife wound but in doing so briefly exposed the inside of his left leg. I jammed the knife as deep as I could into the area adjacent to the groin hoping to catch an artery or large vein. I jerked it out carving upward as I did. He let out a scream and closed up tight in a fetal position. Blood began pouring out of him.

I scooted backward and jumped to my feet, now looking at Teddy. Although he was no longer sitting he had made no effort to help his comrade. He was standing by the chair and had a good size revolver pointed in my direction. He fired and I felt a burning tug as the bullet grazed my right hip. I dove into the hallway for cover feeling trapped as I knew Teddy would only have to take a couple of steps to his left and he would have a clear shot at me. I jumped up and back peddled. Fortunately Teddy did not appear in my line of sight.

I heard Teddy shout at Peter. "If you make any attempt to climb out I will shoot you." Luckily for me, Teddy was torn between staying and keeping Peter prisoner and coming after me.

I was at the end of the hall and opening the door into the garage when he again came into view. I pushed open the door and dove into the garage as the shot rang out. I didn't feel a bullet hit me but the impact with the floor hurt enough. I was tired, hurting and getting a little panicky about my survival chances. I got up and kept moving. I could hear him running behind me.

"Don't let him out of the pit!" Teddy yelled at someone, perhaps the individual with whom I was fighting.

I scrambled to the gap under the garage door and was

just about to dive for it when another shot rang out. The bullet noisily slammed into the aluminum garage door close to my head. Splinters ripped like fire into my face. I jumped away from the opening. He knew my intended way out and had quickly maneuvered to cut me off. Smart kid, I thought, but he should've turned on the lights when he came in the garage. It was even darker in the garage than when I'd come in. If he went back to the light switch he would give me another chance to dive out of the opening. If he pursued me in the dark it improved my odds of getting close enough to him to possibly take away the gun.

Or so I thought. Teddy was a little smarter than I'd assumed. He simply jumped up on the tractor and turned on its headlights. The garage lit up nearly as effectively as if he turned on the overhead lights. With the lights on he saw me at once.

"Who the hell are you?" he asked, pointing the gun at me.

"I'm with the city sewer and water department. Why all the hostility?"

He fired the gun again. I felt the bullet whiz by my left ear. I wasn't sure he meant to miss me. I tried to count how many shots had been fired. He had to be low in ammo with only one or two rounds left.

I leapt behind the tractor and rolled hoping he would fire off his last shot. I knew he had the upper hand but I couldn't just stand there and give him an easy target.

He didn't shoot. Either he knew he was almost out of bullets or he was just being patient. He knew he had trapped me.

"You know I have all day, fool. Who are you really and why are you here?"

"I'm here looking for Melissa Ribbons, the girl that's

gone missing." I answered truthfully, still hiding between the tractor and the garage door. Well, hiding might be stretching it a little. He knew right where I was, I just wanted to keep the tractor between us.

"I don't have the slightest idea who you are talking about. You sure made a big mistake looking for her here, fool."

I believed him but I didn't think he was about to let me go if I said so. He moved directly behind the tractor. I didn't know if he was daring me to make a dash for the gap under the garage door or if he had forgotten about it.

If I stayed still sooner or later he would get an angle on me. I decided to try my luck with the gap. I sprinted and dove for the opening. The impact with the garage floor bruised the bruises I already had on my knees and elbows from my previous collisions with the concrete floor. I heard the shot echo through the interior of the garage and once again slam into the metal door. I was half way through the opening when I realized there was a loud commotion going on behind me -- voices shouting and things banging.

I peeked back and saw two bodies tangled up in a knot rolling around on the floor by the rear of the tractor. One was Peter.

I crawled back in to help. He didn't need it. By the time I got there Peter was slamming Teddy's head into the concrete floor.

"Peter, that's enough. You're going to kill him." He slammed Teddy's unconscious head again into the floor. I reached down and grabbed Peter's shoulder. He wrenched his shoulder free, glaring at me but slowly calming down. Peter had a nasty bruise that had blackened his left eye and put a large knot in the corner of his forehead above the eye.

He looked back down at the limp body and stood up. "I think I did kill him."

I wasn't sure and bent over to feel for a pulse. "He is still alive, but he doesn't look good."

Suddenly a screaming banshee rushed us from behind. It was the girl I had left unconscious in the kitchen. She was yelling and swinging what looked like a meat cleaver as she attacked. Tired and sore, it was all I could do to jump aside. But she was after Peter anyway.

Peter's adrenalin was still pumping. He stepped back and caught her arm as it arced down with the cleaver, twisting it quickly behind her, bringing her wrist almost to the back of her neck. She dropped the weapon in pain and began again with the obscenities.

"Move!" he shouted. With one hand holding her wrist, he used the other to grab the hair on the back of her head guiding her roughly back into the hallway and down towards the room with the pit.

After looking back at Teddy, who was motionless, I followed him into the room. We passed the man I stabbed lying on the floor. I leaned over and felt for a pulse. I couldn't find one. The quantity of blood on the floor around him indicated that I had cut a major vein or artery. I didn't think about him. I would have time later to go through the events of the day.

Peter led her directly to the pit and leaned her towards it. She screamed.

I got my first look into the hole. Two giant rattlesnakes were coiled in the middle of the floor. Dozens of marbles were scattered all over the floor. The pit was about ten feet wide and fifteen feet long. It was only four or five feet deep.

"Shut up or you are going in there!" yelled Peter.

She shut up. I would have too.

Peter looked over at me. "I think my belt is over there on that table along with my other stuff. It should still have my handcuffs. Can you get them for me?"

I hurried over to the table and found the belt, cuffs, everything but his weapon. It reminded me of Joe. I grabbed the cuffs and went back to Peter. He quickly had our prisoner cuffed with her hands behind her back. He sat her down on one of the chairs.

"That bastard and his friends jumped me on the road just east of here. Next thing I knew I came to in this room. They wanted to make sure I was awake when they shoved me into the pit. It was all I could do to stay away from those snakes. A rattlesnake wouldn't naturally have much of an interest in me but Munoz kept antagonizing them."

He reached into the bowl Munoz had been holding and pulled out a large marble, tossing it at one of the snakes. The marble hit the snake. It instantly started rattling and raised its head to a striking position. A second marble missed but landed close and bounced around. The snake started slithering away to get out of the line of fire.

"Munoz kept the snakes mad and moving. I had to keep moving, often getting too close to one or the other of the snakes. They struck at me a number of times. Fortunately I never got that close. But it was only a matter of time. I kept worrying he might shoot me in the leg to slow me down. Luckily you showed up. I owe you a big one." He grinned for the first time since my arrival. "What were you doing here?"

"Long story," I said. "But we need to hurry. Three of his gang took off with one of your fellow deputies after they beat him unconscious. I don't think they were taking him out to get a drink."

"Who was it?" Peter asked.

"Joe," I answered. "I never did get his last name. But an older deputy, more senior in grade I suppose."

"Probably Maldonado, did they say where they were taking him?"

"Not to me," I said, but then had a thought. "But she might know. Think she will tell us?"

In response Peter again lifted her on her feet and pushed her towards the pit. "Where did they take the Deputy?" He asked angrily.

Apparently, she had decided that Peter was bluffing and just yelled some cuss words back in his face.

To my surprise and probably hers, he was not. He shoved her and she had to jump into the pit in order not to simply fall into it. As soon as she landed on the ground both rattlesnakes began rattling. He had pushed her in several feet from the closest rattler. Both snakes coiled up tightly and raised their heads. It was not a pleasant sight.

I knew an American police officer wasn't supposed to behave like this, but Deputy Peter Blanco had had a rough day so I thought I would cut him some slack. Besides, his tactic worked.

"They took him to the old Johnson mine. There is a creek there. They were going to push his car into it."

"Come here," Peter instructed her from the side of the pit.

She edged over to him cautiously, watching the closest snake. When she got to the side Peter reached under her armpits and pulled her back out of the pit. She didn't wise off anymore.

"We need to get someone there quick. Is it far?" I asked.

"About a half hour drive from here. When did they leave?" He was moving over to what looked like a bar counter at the other side of the room. When he got there he reached behind it and pulled out a telephone, dialing as he did.

I looked at my watch. I would have sworn it had been at least an hour. "Just under twenty minutes," I calculated, sitting down in a chair fairly close to our prisoner.

Before anyone answered, Peter looked at me and nodded towards her. "Pay attention," he said to me with a slight grin, "Apache."

At first I thought he might be pulling my leg but then I realized this was home to the Mescalero Indian tribes that were part of the greater Apache tribes in the southwest. I moved my chair a little further away from her.

He contacted his headquarters and recommended they send a helicopter out to the Johnson mine. A car would never make it in time. A helicopter just might. He also requested back up and an ambulance be sent to our location. I was glad he knew where we were.

When he mentioned ambulance, I stood up to go check on Munoz. I suspected the ambulance would be too late. As I stood up, I had to pause and grab a hold of the top of the chair. I felt a little dizzy but not bad.

Peter hung up and I said, "I'd better go check on Munoz."

"Okay," he replied. "But I didn't call the ambulance for him."

I walked out to check on Munoz. He was where we left him, the pool of blood around his head a little bigger. I reached over and felt his pulse. Surprisingly, he still had one.

I walked back towards the others and paused at the darkened room. I flicked on the lights. It had a desk and a set of bunk beds in it. Some men's clothing had been thrown messily on the floor and on the lower bunk.   There was nothing really unusual. It was probably a room where workmen crashed during the night. There was a mirror in the room so I walked into the room to take a look at myself. I looked worse than I felt. That would probably come later. Somewhere in the melee, I'd received a number of small cuts to the side of my face, probably from the ricochet. A lot of blood had run down my face onto my neck and shirt. My lip was puffed up and looked ugly. My jeans had a dark black blotch around a tear on my hip where the bullet had creased me and the blood had run.   I knew that wound was superficial.

I crossed over into the kitchen and grabbed the platter of sliced sausage. Peering into the refrigerator I saw our options were either beer or coke. I wanted the first but figured with people showing up any minute we'd better stick with the cokes. I grabbed two and took them along with some sausage out to Peter.

"Hungry?" I asked as I entered the room.

He was sitting close to her. They were talking, peacefully, for a change.

He got up pointed to the bar, and I placed the sausage and cokes on it.

"Thanks," he said as he grabbed one of the cokes. "Now that I think of it, I'm starving."

"Your body is getting back to normal. Are you okay?" I asked.

"My head hurts but otherwise I'm fine. You know, I know that girl. At least I know her family. Her brother is a friend of mine. His name is Martin, Martin Alvarado. We use to hang out together in high school. She's his little sister Consuela. I told her who I was and that she should be ashamed of herself. I know her parents. They are good people. I bet they have no idea she has been hanging out here. Martin will be furious when he finds out. He's in the Marines right now but is due to be getting out next spring. Been to Iraq and has some medals. You know the Marines will pay for his college. The family is so proud of him and what does his little sister do but bring the family back down."

"She is still young, and may not be too deeply involved with all this," I said, not believing it myself. "She may just be a recent girlfriend of one of the guys."

"Yeah, Munoz," Peter said with disgust.

I looked back over at Consuela. I never could understand why so many women found bad guys attractive.

The sound of an ambulance siren drifted into the room. Peter walked over to Consuela and helped her to her feet, holding her arm. He looked at me, "Let's go outside and wait for it. I need some fresh air."

"Okay, but give me a minute, I want to check on Munoz again." Peter walked out the door to the outside and I returned to the garage. Munoz hadn't moved. I didn't check for a pulse. I guess I didn't care. I was tired and this was still going to be long day. Questions to be answered, statements to be written and doctors poking and prodding my already sore body.

I realized that I hadn't seen the gun Munoz fired at me since the fighting ended. I didn't think Peter had it. I looked around for it and saw it under the tractor about eight feet from where Munoz lay. Perhaps not the best tactic leaving a weapon close to a person who had just fired it at you, but I didn't think Munoz would be using it and I didn't feel like crawling under the tractor to retrieve it. I walked back out to the front entrance and onto the parking lot where Peter and Consuela stood talking. They both had calmed down a lot. I was glad as she could make an excellent witness. It would be beneficial to her and to us.

Judging from the sound of the siren, the ambulance was almost on top of us but the trees and underbrush blocked the view of most of the driveway and of the road beyond.

I glanced back at Consuela. She was an attractive young woman, when she wasn't swinging at you with a meat cleaver. She also looked thinner than I'd first realized. Peter had thrown one of the men's jackets over her shoulders but it hung open in the front.

We were standing in one of the last patches of sunlight as the sun was trying to disappear behind the mountains. Despite the cold temperature, the sun was warm at this altitude, close to seven thousand five hundred feet. It would get really cold once the sun dropped behind the mountains. I thought again of Melissa.

"Consuela, do you know or have you heard of a Melissa Ribbons?" I asked as the ambulance finally came in view and turned off its siren. Two sheriff's cruisers were right behind it.

"The girl that's missing?" she asked.

"Yes."

"No, I have never seen her and I don't know where she is." She answered so easily that I believed her. I had not given much credence to the theory the Teddy might have been involved in her disappearance. But I could see why Peter had his suspicions after seeing what Teddy was capable of today.

The medics on the ambulance took a cursory look at Peter and me, but at our prompting went in to do what they could for Munoz and the other person inside. I couldn't believe it but Munoz was still alive. His partner wasn't as lucky.

Sergeant Morrison and another city cop showed up a minute or two after the others. They were out of their jurisdiction but came to provide additional support. More than likely they were a bit curious too. In this small town there usually wasn't this much excitement.

It seemed to me everyone was more interested in viewing the snake pit than doing much police work.

Sergeant Morrison came back out of the building and approached me. "They've agreed to have me take you back to the city hospital. The docs there will clean and patch you up. They will get a statement from you tomorrow. Looks like you've had a rough day."

I was ready to leave and got into Morrison's police vehicle for the second time that day. As we started to pull out of the parking lot I saw Consuela sitting in the back seat of one of the Deputy's vehicles. Someone in a white jeep pulled off the driveway into the parking area just as we pulled onto it.

"Looks like the press is here," mumbled Morrison.

"Sergeant, what's the latest on Deputy Maldonado?"

"They found him and his car in the streambed near the Johnson mine. It was supposed to look like an accident although I can't imagine how somebody would end up down there. Not near any working roads. If the Sheriff's office didn't know where to look, he may not have been found until someone stumbled upon the scene by accident.

Who knows when that would have been?"

Interrupting, I asked. "But is he okay?"

"Don't know for sure.   All any of us know was he was alive when they found him but he was in real bad shape. The helicopter guys that located him took him directly to Roswell to the big hospital.   Did you see the guys responsible?"

"Not very clearly but I know two of their names, Pico and Julio. Peter was there longer than I was. He may have a better idea who the three are."

Morrison got on the radio and passed the names onto the county and to his city office. "I'm not sure how much they know," he said. "They have a surveillance set up around the property watching for them to come back. I guess they were supposed to go back to the warehouse after they got rid of Joe."

I was happy to hear that Joe had a chance. I knew if they could get him to the hospital in time the odds were pretty good.

The drive back into town went quickly. We must have only been a mile or so from city limits. Once into town I noticed the city streetlights were going on. It had indeed been a long day. We drove by the Brown Bear Inn and the bank with the flashing temperature. Thirty six degrees, it hadn't seemed that cold.

The rest of the afternoon and early evening were slow and painful for me. Painful not just because of the stitches I received but because more time went by without my getting to the work I was supposed to be doing, which was making some kind of progress in determining what happened to Melissa.

Chapter 9

The hospital was really just a large clinic with minimal rooms for inpatients. I didn't plan on needing one anyway. But it was clean and the staff was friendly. A number of different people came in and out of the treatment room they placed me in but I don't think any of them were doctors. All my wounds were superficial and simply required some cleansing and closing. Only my hip needed a few stitches and they were put in place by an elderly nurse or technician who kept chastising me.

"How can a man your age still find ways to get into fights? Seems silly to me."

I didn't argue with her.

Before they sent me on my way, I was given a prescription for antibiotics. Infection would be the only threat I had to deal with now. Take them all as prescribed they instructed and told me a drugstore was conveniently located across the street.

I had already told Sergeant Morrison that I could easily walk back to my hotel and he left shortly after our arrival at the clinic. I felt somewhat refreshed and a little cleaner, but I still needed a shower. Getting back into my clothes was a downer as they were dirty, torn, and bloodstained. I should have suggested we stop by the hotel so I could have gotten a change of clothes while in route to the hospital.

Despite my appearance, I walked across the street to the

drug store and headed straight to the pharmacy. There was only one person in line ahead of me, a man, maybe in his mid sixties. I noticed he already had his little bag in his hand and he was just chatting with the pharmacist, another man about the same age. I sat there patiently.

Fortunately, just after a minute or two of waiting the pharmacist looked over at me. I must have looked pretty sad because I could hear him tell his friend that he had better go so he could take care of me. As he referred to me, he pointed and the customer looked over at me. They both stared for a second and the customer said something like I see and headed off. I walked up to the counter.

"What happened to you, sir?"

"Oh, just an accident," I said handing him the prescription.

"Sorry to keep you waiting," he remarked as he turned and went back to his shelves of various pills and potions.

"No problem, I know it's always nice to get a chance to visit with old friends."

I heard him chuckle to himself and then turn back to me with a container he was putting into a small brown bag.

"Well I guess he is an old friend. Married my wife. Did me a favor." He chuckled to himself again. "Of course that was nearly forty years ago."

"You all get along now?"

"Sure, but I don't see much of them anymore. Besides she has really changed since the loss of their daughter. He says she is withdrawn and just sulks around all day. This time of the year is the worst seeing how her daughter went missing right around now seven or so years ago. It took days to find her. She had fallen off a ledge not far from their backyard and died. Snow buried her till they found her.

Yeah this time of year she always needs a lot of sedatives so she can sleep." The old pharmacist rambled on. At first I was just talking to be nice and could care less about him or his prior customer. With the mention of the daughter I began listening intently.

"So she was the first of the missing girls?" I asked.

"First? No, sadly we've had boys, girls, men, women and pets go missing around here come winter time. Sad thing it is. Luckily it doesn't happen that often but it has been happening as far back as I can remember. I remember just after the war a nasty spring storm trapped a number of fishermen in a camp over by Cloudcroft. Eleven people died. This is beautiful country sir but never trust it."

I decided interviewing the pharmacist was not a good idea. His comments put my focus back where it belonged but I doubted if he had much more to add. I thanked him and walked back outside. It was getting colder and there was a breeze coming out of the northwest. I walked quickly back to the hotel.

No one was in the lobby. I proceeded straight to my room threw all my dirty clothes into a pile on the floor and jumped into the shower. The room had felt cold, too. I needed a hot shower and stood there longer than my Mom would have ever allowed. Hopefully there was no water shortage in Ruidoso. I had to organize in my mind what all happened today and file it away for tomorrow. Then, and more importantly, I needed to get my mind back towards developing a better strategy to accomplish what I came down here to do. Find out what happened to Melissa.

I did realize that we had at least eliminated one possible suspect, perhaps in more ways than one. It didn't bring me any closer to the answer but it did slightly narrow the field.

However, I still needed to develop some viable leads to pursue. Just keep trying to eliminate suspects and you may just end up with a winner. Persistency was so important in cases like this, just as it is in solving any cold case. I developed a mental plan of action for the morning and turned off the shower about the same time the reservoir hit its low water mark.

I put on all clean clothes. That is a different pair of jeans, an old Duke sweatshirt and some work boots. Good enough for the Mescalero Café I thought. I also put on my heavier jacket.

Crossing the street I noticed the temperature was already down to twenty eight degrees. The wind was still blustery. It felt really cold but the warmth from the shower stayed with me to the café.

It was a little late for dinner but I could see the restaurant was still open and customers were visible through the windows. I walked in and went directly to an empty table. Most were.

A young waitress, one I had not seen earlier in the day was at the table as soon as I sat down. "Howdy Mister, welcome to the Mescalero Café, can I get you a drink?"

She looked like she was barely out of high school. Her left arm had a multi-color tattoo that appeared to cover the whole arm above the elbow. I couldn't tell what it was due to the sleeve and my barely successful effort not to stare at it. "Can I get a beer here?"

"Sure, Bud, Bud Light, Miller, Miller Lite. All bottled, nothing on tap." She smiled and then did something with her tongue and teeth. I noticed her tongue had been pierced and had some silver thing on it.

"A Bud Light will be fine."

"I'll be right back with your drink." She walked away towards the counter.

I looked around in the restaurant. An older man was eating by himself by the window watching the traffic go by. A group of four middle aged ladies were together at another table by the counter. They were looking at me. They looked as though they had finished eating and were just visiting. They kept looking at me.

Another younger couple, maybe mid-twenties, was at the table next to the door that led to the back room. I couldn't tell if they had already eaten or not. They were also looking at me, but looked away as I looked at them.

I looked down at myself. I hadn't forgotten my pants, shoes, or anything else.

"You know you are a bit of a celebrity in town." A voice said behind me. It was Kristi. She was wearing black jeans and a thick blue pullover sweater with a blue and silver scarf tied around her neck.

"You look nice," I said automatically.

"Thanks."

"What makes me a celebrity? And how would anyone recognize me?"

She grinned. "I could just ask if you've looked at your face recently."

I had forgotten about my swollen lip and cut up cheek.

"That bad?"

"No, it's not that bad. I think it gives you character." Another grin, "Actually it was all over the evening news tonight."

"What was?" I asked, although I had a feeling I knew.

"Your rescue of Deputy Blanco, helping to save Deputy Maldonado, someone getting killed, the rattlesnakes, something about drugs, a manhunt still going on out there, and finally Teddy Munoz, the son of one of our wealthier citizens being in intensive care. This is normally a peaceful place so that kind of story gets everyone's attention. Most people in town know one of the people mentioned. Throw in the rattlesnakes and you couldn't have made up a better way to get people's attention. I bet most everyone in a fifty mile radius will be watching the ten o'clock news tonight."

"I figured it would be on the news. But why would anyone recognize me. Certainly they didn't have a picture of me on the news."

"Not yet, but I bet they are looking for one. Actually, your fame may not be that wide spread yet. Don't get mad at Rose and Daisy but when the story broke on the six o'clock news, they both happened to be here and they may have over stated their familiarity with you to a few of the regular customers. You have been staying at the Brown Bear Inn and eating here at the café. With Rose and Daisy that almost makes you family. A lot of the customers were understandably interested. Like I said this type of stuff never happens here. The couple over there and the gals at that table arrived shortly before Daisy left with her sister. If you ask me they were all hanging around in case you showed up. Daisy said you would."

As if to prove Kristi's statement the ladies got up to leave.

"I certainly don't need the publicity. I still have a lot to do."

"Well, for what it's worth, I think you've already done a lot today. I don't really know what all happened, it all sounded confusing to me, but I imagine a lot of people in this county appreciate what you've done. That includes me,

I know both those deputies."

"Here's your beer, sir." The tattooed young girl had returned. "Hi Kristi, are you joining him?" The kid had a smile that looked like a smirk to me.

"If you aren't busy please sit down," I offered.

"Okay, but just for a few minutes. I've already eaten."

"Can I get you a drink?" The waitress asked.

"No, I'm fine."

"You ready to order, sir?"

I just ordered a hamburger and probably stared too long, just out of curiosity, at the waitress as she walked back towards the kitchen.

"She's a character," commented Kristi.

"I know it's the fad now, but I don't understand why anyone would want to get something pierced through their tongue, or paint up their arm like that, or wear more than a half a dozen ear rings on one ear."

"That tattoo covers up most everything above her waistline, back and front. Stops at her neck and the other shoulder. It's actually quite a work of art but why she had it done I'll never understand either."

"Luckily I don't have any kids," I said.

"She's the granddaughter of one of Daisy's close friends. In the kid's defense, she is actually a very nice person and a dependable worker."

"Kristi, you mentioned earlier that on the news they mentioned something about Deputy Joe Maldonado. What was his condition?"

"They reported his condition as critical but stable, I think. He is in the ICU over at Roswell with a severe head injury. I'm sure they will update his condition on the ten o'clock news."

We both sat in silence for a few seconds. I didn't have much small talk left in me and I knew it was too early in our relationship for me just to grab her by her hand and walk her over to my hotel room.

She broke the silence.   "You know there are other restaurants in town.   There's a nice steak house just around the corner.   If you are still in town tomorrow night why don't you let me buy you dinner?"

"Sounds good," I replied, and it did. "I suspect I'll be in town for at least the next two to three days. I'm not sure of my schedule but say around seven?"

"Seven's good.   Just meet me here and we can walk over." She stood up smiling. "I need to run and take care of a few things, see you tomorrow." She turned and left the restaurant.

The beer tasted good. There were no other customers in the restaurant now. I imagined it was nearing their closing time. Larry was at the register studying something. He looked up at me and nodded. I nodded back.

The young waitress showed up with my hamburger. "If this isn't done just right for you, sir, let me know and we'll fix it."

Well, she was polite and efficient, I thought. I told her I was sure it would be fine and caught myself staring at her again as she walked back to the kitchen. That tattoo had grabbed more of my interest.

Chapter 10

I tried to stay awake for the ten o'clock news. In fact the clock said it was five minutes before ten when I crawled into bed. Unfortunately it was then that I discovered that the television remote was sitting next to the television out of reach. I lay there contemplating my strategy on getting out of bed and to the remote. The next thing I knew a truck down shifted somewhere outside my room and woke me up. It was seven thirty in the morning.

I needed to get up but at the same time I had an urge to call the mayor and complain about the early morning truck noises in the city.

I got up, skipped shaving and got dressed. Same jeans as I wore the night before but a different sweatshirt, this one said Baylor. My mid weight jacket was a disaster so I was stuck with the heavy one.

I walked out into the lobby. The coffee smell was there again. So was Rose this time.

"Good morning, Mr. West. Would you like some coffee?"

"Sure, Rose," I thought her hair was pinker today. "It smells good."

Rose disappeared into the office behind the counter and emerged moments later carrying with a mug of coffee. "Here it is Mr. West, on the house."

As I thanked her and reached for the mug, I heard another voice.

"Good morning Jim, I thought you might like some brownies this morning." The voice was Marge's from the boutique. She was dressed in a pair of tight slacks and a sweater that exposed about an inch of her waistline above her pants. It was cut low in the front, too, exposing even more. Her hair looked a little lighter than it was yesterday. She was carrying a plate of chocolate frosted brownies.

"We're all so grateful for what you've done to save those boys with the Sheriff's department. It must have been frightening." Marge gently grabbed my arm by the elbow as she said frightening and inched closer to me.

If I was on an airplane, I would have been looking for the emergency exits by now. Peter's comments about her were obviously not exaggerated.

"Why thank you Marge, I'll have one. They look delicious but I'll need to eat it on the run. I promised the authorities I would report in to them first thing this morning."

"Oh, nobody is up doing anything yet this morning. It's barely eight. Come sit down and tell me all about how you saved that young detective from those rattlesnakes." She still had a hold on my arm and backed towards a couch that she had already dumped her coat on at one end. She was aiming towards the middle and supposedly I was to be snuggled in next to her and the open end of the couch.

I wasn't moving.

"Marge, don't be pestering Mr. West so," Rose said coming to my rescue. "You'll make him spill his coffee."

"All right, I don't mean any harm," she said with a smile. "Maybe I'll call you a little later, Mr. West. There are a lot of nice things to do and see around here and I wouldn't mind being the one to show you around."

"Well thank you Marge, but I have no idea what my schedule will be the next couple of days." I finished the brownie. "Thanks again for the brownie, but I must be going." I took a big drink of coffee, almost burning my mouth, returned the mug to the counter and said my good-byes.

"Make sure you have your key," was Rose's only comment.

Marge actually said "Ta-ta" and raised her hand in a little wave. They say a coyote will chew off its own leg to get out of a trap. I was beginning to believe it.

Outside, I noticed that the wind was still out of the northwest. Low clouds covered the sky and a light snowfall had already begun. The bank's sign said it was twenty seven degrees. Despite my heavy jacket, it felt colder. I walked to the city police station.

It wasn't a long walk and as I entered the building I was greeted by a young, tall, lanky officer I didn't know. "Is Sergeant Morrison in today?" I asked.

"Not yet, but he should be here any minute. Can I do anything for you or would you like to wait?"

"I'll wait. Thanks." I moved to one of the couches. On the table in front of the couch sat a local paper. I checked the date and it was today's paper. The front page had three photos on it along with the story. The pictures were of Peter, Maldonado, and Munoz. I was just starting to read the article when Morrison walked in.

"Good morning, Jim, how are you feeling this morning?"

"Actually, pretty good, the clinic verified that all the wounds were superficial. They look worse than they are."

"Glad to hear it. What can we do for you today?" He asked.

"Two things, can you contact the Sheriff's office and see if they want me to make a statement. If they do and I imagine they will, see if I can do it here to one of their deputies or to you. Secondly, I'd like to look again at anything at all that you can find regarding the earlier incidents with the girls that died. The Sheriff's office may have more and I can call Deputy Blanco when we get done here."

"I don't think we have anything more than what you saw yesterday, but I'll double check. When I call the sheriff's office to see where they would like you to work up the statement, I'll see what else they might have on the earlier cases."

"Thanks," I said.

"While you are waiting would you like a cup of coffee?"

"Sure, if it's already made. Thanks."

"It is," and turning to the Officer behind the desk, "Buddy, will you get this man a cup of coffee."

Buddy disappeared down the hall.

"Jim, anything you need in this matter, trying to find the missing girl, work it directly with me. That is any work with the city police. I know you also need to work it with the county. I did some thinking last night and I think you have a point. There is something fishy about all the girls looking so much alike. I know it's a common look with the young gals but this is more than just a coincidence."

"Thanks, Rick, I appreciate that."

Buddy returned with the coffee.

"Buddy, this here's Jim West. He's the man that helped out yesterday with the Sheriff's office and all that stuff that happened just outside of town. He'll be using the conference room this morning to review some files on those girls that went missing and were later found dead the last few years. We will be having some files brought over from the sheriff's office. If I'm not here, make sure they get to him."

Buddy said he would. Rick and I walked down the hall and up some stairs to the second floor. The small conference room was adjacent to the stairway. It wasn't much larger than a normal size office and simply consisted of a large rectangular wooden table surrounded by twelve chairs. The wall opposite the doorway had another ten or so chairs lined up against it and at the far end of the table stood a podium.

"We won't be using this room today so you should have plenty of room to spread out. Give me a few minutes and I'll get our files again and I'll call over to the sheriff's office. Make yourself at home. Our Captain's office is just down the hall so he may pop in. I'll let his secretary know you are here." Rick left me there.

I took off my coat and took a seat near the door. I really didn't expect much more from the city's files as I had seen a lot of what they had yesterday. I was hoping, however, that the sheriff's files might have some hidden nugget that could help me discover what had happened to Melissa.

"So, are you the famous Mr. West?" A pleasant sounding voice said from the doorway.

I looked up. A very attractive lady, maybe in her mid thirties, tall, brunette with dark eyes stood in the doorway. She was wearing a dark blue pants suit.

"I guess infamous may be a better word." I said as I stood up.

"I'm Sharon Cane," she said as she put out her hand. I took it. "I'm Captain Marshall's secretary. Rick told me you were here, so I had to come and see who everyone has been talking about this morning. You know we have had calls from the television station, the paper and the radio people wanting to know how to get in touch with you."

I shook my head. "The last thing I want or need is to have any contact with them. I hope you didn't tell them I was here."

"Don't worry, we didn't and won't. You know it's not like the cops to ever share credit anyway, or infer they can't take care of themselves. Especially with the election coming up, I doubt if Sheriff Mendez wants any type of news implying some outsider had to save a bunch of his deputies." She paused for a second, staring at me. "I understand you are looking for Melissa Ribbons. Hope you find her. I see you have coffee, if you need anything else just come down and ask." She smiled at me again, turned and walked back down the hallway.

I stood there for a few minutes trying to refocus on to what I was there to do. Across the hall, a young blond lady in a police uniform came out of a door with the word DISPATCH written across the front. She nodded at me and walked down the hall towards the Captain's office. I tried not to stare after her, all the while wondering how many Miss New Mexico's had come from this little town.

I went back to my chair about the same time Rick came back in with a pile of folders that looked not much bigger than the one I had gone through yesterday.

"I think you read most of these already, but that's all we have. Good news though, I called Deputy Blanco and he will be bringing over everything he can get his hands on. He thought he would be here in an hour."

"How is he doing?" I asked. "He went through a lot yesterday. He should be taking a few days off."

"He sounded fine, other than that I don't know."

"Have you heard anything more on Deputy Maldonado?"

"Yes, the latest report is that he is stable, talking and they think he should make a full recovery."

I was glad to hear that. While the press might be playing up my role in his rescue, I personally felt a little guilty for just standing there behind the trees watching them take him away.

We went through the files again page by page discussing what few possible leads might still be left to follow. There didn't appear to be much to go on. We were debating the value of my calling the families of the former victims when Peter walked in carrying a large briefcase. He was dressed in jeans, cowboy boots and a heavy flannel shirt.

"Good to see you this morning, Mr. West and Sergeant Morrison." His bruise had darkened a lot around his eye and temple.

"How are you doing today, Peter?" I asked.

"I have a bit of a headache, but other than that I feel fine. The county has me on admin leave for the next few days, but that is normal. It will give me more time to work on this with you." Peter pulled out the files and put them on the table. "And did you hear? Joe is going to be just fine."

"Rick just told me that. That's good to know. How about Teddy?"

"They have him stabilized, but he is still critical and the docs aren't too optimistic. His Dad is starting to raise some cane. He called the Sheriff and told him to get back here now. He also called the governor and said he wants an outside inquiry. The DA is pretty good friends with him though, and he said later today he will sit down with him and make sure he understands all the facts. The DA says he'll come around. Teddy has always been a pain for the old man. He's got two other older sons and an older daughter who have all done good. By the way, someone will be over here later this morning to get a statement from you, Mr. West. They told me to tell you to stay put."

"No problem, it will take us a while to get through the paperwork you brought over."

For the next two hours we scrutinized the details of the old reports. Nothing at all jumped out at us as a hot lead. I was beginning to feel depressed. There were several more pictures of each of the girls. Some had been supplied by families and some by friends that were with them skiing. Close up pictures of the girls did disclose distinguishing features for each, but again I was struck how similar each of the girls looked in any picture taken a dozen or so feet away from them. Put them in a ski jacket with a stocking cap on their heads and they looked even more like each other.

Both Rick and Peter seemed now to be on my side. The similarity in the girls' appearances and the same way and time of the year the girls went missing discredited the coincidence theory. We studied the pictures and verified all the other people in any picture taken while they were here had been interviewed. One picture brought the similarities to home for all of us. A picture in the Stephanie Bridges file showed three girls standing side by side on one of the slopes at Ski Apache. All three girls had on matching white ski pants, jackets and gloves. One wore a green stocking cap, one a white one and one cap was red. Each cap had what looked like a yellow star on the front of it. Any of the three girls could have passed for any of the victims. The back of the picture was annotated to point out the girl in the red cap was Stephanie and the other two were her younger twin sisters.

We also plotted the discovery location of each of the girls. Although none of the discoveries were in the immediate vicinity of any of the others, they all were located on the lower portion of the mountain that was home to Ski Apache. Rick and Peter said that only made sense as the majority of the cross country ski trails and hiking trails were on the eastern face of the mountain. The main ski area was on the northern face and the west and southern portions pressed against the rest of the mountain range. People lost back there may not be discovered for years.

"Is there a way to move along a trail or a ridge line that interconnects above all these locations?" I asked.

"Not a single trail," answered Peter right away. "But many of the footpaths and ski trails do intersect and if you knew your way around you can go quite a distance in any direction. There is a lot of private property that you aren't supposed to cross, but nobody really cares. I've done a lot of hiking up there. It's rough though, I wouldn't want to try it in a snow storm or in the dark."

"Another question that has been nagging me is why would any of these girls go up into that mountain side just to fall off? I know a couple of the girls were staying up at the lodge up there, but the others were staying down at the lower elevations like Melissa. I can believe she wandered off and got lost but why go up the mountain when you are trying to find your way back?"

Rick answered this question. "That's a good point but there are a couple logical explanations. First none of them had to go up the mountain. If you approach the side of the mountain from the east in the dark and then try to go in any other direction you can easily fall into a shallow ravine, runoff area, or crevice and hit your head hard enough to knock yourself out. A ten foot fall could do it. The cold would do the rest and quickly. Second, there is a bar or two hidden back there in the foothills. A lot of the locals hike to them rather than drive. If you still have daylight or even a full moon, or you really know what you are doing it's not too hard to hike to them. The Backwoods Bar mentioned in the Phyllis girl's file, the place she was last seen is one of them. Buck's Hideout is the other. There used to be a third until the owner died early this year, The Tick. Remember that place Peter?"

"Sure do, that place was wild. I did ask the employees at both the bars if they had seen Melissa and neither place had any knowledge of her at all."

"Do many people live up there above where the bodies were later discovered?"

Peter took this question, "There are about a dozen homes up there that are occupied year round. There are maybe another ten to fifteen homes where people spend part of the year here. Then there are a number of run down places where no one resides any more. Most of those are on private property. They are just empty and run down."

I started to ask if they all had direct access to the side of the mountain and realized that was a dumb question since they all lived on the side of the mountain. "If we went out there and plotted the likely places where each of these girls may have fallen, if we assume they fell off the mountainside, would any of the private property be situated on those spots?"

Both Peter and Rick studied the map we had spread out on the table. "Only a couple," Peter advised. He looked at

Rick, "You know the Hamilton's live up there. Their daughter was this girl here," he reached over and grabbed the newspaper article that had the picture of the five dead girls and Melissa. "She was the first. But she was local and we are sure her fall was an accident."

"There was no file, no investigation on her?" I asked.

"No, but there were sufficient witnesses and circumstances to verify it was just an accident. It took days to find her though." Peter explained. "It was her birthday and a couple of friends were at her house along with her parents. They were going to have a party for her later that night. It was snowing quite heavily and windy. She went out back to try out some new skis on the trail behind her house. She told her parents she would only be out for a couple of minutes. When she never came in, her Mom and the friends went out to look for her. Even with the snow falling they could track her trail in the snow for about seventy five yards. The trail stopped and they found one ski. No sign of any other presence, animal or human. Best guess was that she stopped to adjust a binding and she slipped or something gave way under her and she slid off the side of the mountain. There is a big drop off there and depending how she fell, she could have been propelled in a couple of different directions. The face of the mountain is fairly inaccessible there and it snowed very hard the rest of that day and the next. I believe it was almost a week later when they finally found her body about seventy five yards below where she fell, stuck in a jagged crevice and covered with snow."

They pointed out the Hamilton's place on the map. "The Acorns live just over here and the Gables up here." Peter elaborated. "None of the other properties have ready access to the ridgeline. Most of it is national park and anyone can get access to it if they want."

"Peter, could you take me up there today. I'd like to get a better feel for what it's like along there."

"We could do it after lunch, if you like. I'm off anyways today and you've stirred up my curiosity.   I don't think anyone has plotted all of the likely places each of the victims could have fallen from and then compared them to each other."

We continued discussing other possibilities and at ten thirty two deputies showed up to take my statement. Rick left the room to see what was going on downstairs. Peter said he was going to run an errand and that he would be back in an hour.

They took statements differently than I was used to. Rather than have me write down in my own words what took place, they had a series of questions already typed out on separate pages and had me write out the answers. Why did I go to the warehouse? Who was at the warehouse? What did I see at the warehouse? And seven more questions that were similar to them. I guess it kept me to the point but also left out a lot of relevant issues that someone with a mind to could omit. I didn't and I ignored the few comments that I didn't need to be so detailed. All in all, I wasn't too impressed with their effort. I definitely got the opinion that they thought Teddy would never last for a trial and the three fugitives would either never be seen again or might not survive long enough to go to trial either. I had some empathy for them. These guys had tried to kill two of their own. But still it lacked a little professionalism. They never told me the name of the man I had killed. I never asked.

Peter showed back up when I was on my last question. Had I seen Teddy shoot at anyone? That was an easy one.

They asked Peter to stay and for me to step down stairs to the lobby as they had something they wanted to discuss with him alone. Leaving the room, I looked down the hall and saw that the door to the Captain's office was closed. I went downstairs.

Chapter 11

The lobby was empty except for a man in hunting fatigues complaining to Rick and Buddy about a traffic ticket he had gotten the night before. They all ignored me and I sat and waited for Peter. I didn't have to wait long before the three deputies walked into the lobby. I noticed one of the other deputies now had the briefcase that Peter had brought with him that morning.

"Thank you Mr. West. Hopefully that will be all that we will need," said the older of the two as they left.

"Guess what?" asked Peter.

"What?" I answered, I didn't feel like guessing.

"They found some stuff that belonged to a guy found dead this past August in a field about ten miles east of here. He died from a couple of rattlesnake bites. The guy had only been in town a few months. It was considered a suspicious death as no one knew how he got out to where he was found. No car, bike or anything was found close to him. We found out he had been in and out of jail a lot in Arizona, mostly juvenile stuff, but still not a nice guy. The new theory is that Teddy and his boys may have been involved with his death. Because of that, they want to take a closer look at all the investigations on the missing girls to see if there may be a link."

"I don't think he was involved." I said.

"Me, either, not anymore," Peter added. "After how you

said he answered your question about Melissa and after talking to Teddy's girlfriend Consuela, I'm fairly certain that he wasn't involved with them. You know she has opened up a lot. Consuela will put the nail in his coffin if Satan doesn't take him first."

"Well I'm glad she's talking. Hopefully the DA won't be too hard on her if she cooperates. If we're done here, let's go someplace remote and grab a bite to eat and then drive up to that area above where the girls were found."

"Sure, let's go, but why do you say remote?" Peter asked.

"Rick mentioned he had some calls by the press about me. I'd rather not run into any of them. Secondly, Marge showed up early this morning at the hotel with brownies. She wants to show me some of the city highlights. I'm pretty sure I don't want to see them."

Peter chuckled. "Sorry man, but you are not safe anywhere around here now. She has her spies everywhere. You may just have to give in to her, could be worse."

I ignored Peter's attempt at humor and asked Buddy if he could retrieve the map and the newspaper page with the six girls' pictures from the conference room table. The deputies had left the city's files and I thought those two items would be all that we needed anyway. Rick came over and wished us good luck as we left the building.

Peter pointed out his car to me. It was a small red Chevy. "We can grab something at one of those places we mentioned and I'll show you what Rick was trying to explain to you about people walking to them."

I imagined he meant one of the remote bars in the woods. I didn't remember the names but anyplace out of town was fine with me.

We drove for about five minutes towards Nocelo and Ski Apache and turned off on a narrow side road that took us slowly up the base of the mountain. We drove about a half of a mile and turned back towards Ruidoso on a dirt road that wound through forest and hills. Our pace was slow as the condition of the road was bad. I was afraid at a couple of spots Peter might bottom out his car. After traveling about three or four minutes, we turned down a short driveway and around a clump of trees and parked in front of an old wooden building. The building definitely looked as though it had seen better days. A wooden porch spanned the front of the building and I imagined in the summer customers might even sit out on it. There was only one other car in the parking lot. A hand painted sign that was nailed across some of the front porch railings said Backwoods Bar. Just after the word Bar, were the words "and Grill" painted in much smaller print.

"Safe to eat here?" I asked with a smile.

"They have good hamburgers, chili, that kind of stuff," he responded and led me into the restaurant.

The place looked empty, but as my eyes adjusted to the darkness of the restaurant I saw there were two men eating something at a table at the far end of the room. A big bearded guy in the typical lumberjack's red and black flannel shirt came out from what I guessed was the kitchen, saw us and told us to sit anywhere we want. That gave us a choice of the ten or so picnic tables or one of the dozen stools that lined the bar. We took the picnic table nearest us.

The big guy turned out to also be our waiter. "What can I get for you?"

Peter looked at me, "I don't think they have menus."

"That's right, no lunch menus," he confirmed. "We do

what we can to cut down on overhead. We got hot dogs, hamburgers, our specialty today is venison chili. Homemade," he said with a grin, "we throw the venison sausage in the chili ourselves."

"Give me a couple hot dogs and a beer," I said.

"Me too," stated Peter.

"Dos Equis, okay?" asked the big guy. "That's what I've been drinking."

"Sure," I responded, "and put it on one tab for me."

"Big spender," he said and walked away.

"I wouldn't want to get that guy mad at me."

"Me neither," Peter echoed. "Let me show you something on this map." He unfolded the map on the table. "Here we are. As you can see, Ruidoso city line is less than a mile from here. Nocelo over here is more like three miles as a crow flies. The victims were all found along here and where we are going next, up here," he drew his finger over the map as he was pointing out each area. "Again, as a crow flies none of these areas are more than a couple of miles from here. It's just we can't fly so we'll need to drive back out to the main road, turn off on the road to Ski Apache, and then take this first side road that goes over and up to the area where we want to go today."

We talked some more before our lunch came. The hot dogs came with a handful of potato chips and a dill pickle slice. The big guy also brought us a tray containing plastic containers of pickle relish, onions and mustard. Ketchup was already on the table.

"Might I suggest the onions" he said and lumbered away.

"Don't worry," Peter said, "the beer will kill the germs."

As we left the bar, Peter led me out to the far end of the

small parking lot and showed me where a footpath left the parking lot and disappeared around some trees. "That trail will take you back to the city. Maybe a thirty minute walk. There are a few others that weave their way in here. One joins the driveway opposite of the road we came in on and two others run off the end of the restaurant over there. They head in the direction of the mountain and where we are going next."

"How long would it take us to walk up into the area?"

"Well you can't really walk to where we are going. Both trails will get you close but unless you want to do some real climbing you still have to go around. One of the trails takes you deep into the mountain to a series of lakes and camping areas west of where we want to go. The other gets us real close and then veers northeast along the base of the steeper slopes and goes all the way back out to the highway."

We got back into Peter's car and began the slow drive back out to the main road. Going back seemed quicker. Once on the main road we turned away from Ruidoso and continued towards the Ski Apache exit. It only took a few minutes and when we arrived at the exit, we turned to the left in the direction of the ski area. The road immediately began to climb up the mountainside. It was a pretty drive but within the first mile we again turned left onto the road that would take us to our destination. We immediately descended a little before flattening out and then as the road curved back to the right we started to climb again.

Peter stopped the car and we got out. "Come over here, let me show you something."

I walked about twenty yards with him to a vantage point where we could see a large expanse of the surrounding area. It was a pretty view.

"There is the road we were just on." I could easily see the road and the traffic on it. "Ruidoso is over there. You can't quite see it because the land rises right in front of it. Those buildings over there are in Nocelo. Pretty much make up the whole town. Back there is where we had lunch. You can't see the restaurant but see that smoke, I imagine it may be coming up off the grill. The slope here is still pretty mild but as we go up further the slope on this side really falls off. I'll show you."

We walked back to the car and continued our uphill drive. The first residence we came to belonged to the Hamilton's. We drove by it and in another half mile passed the second. It looked vacant. Shortly past the second residence the road curved right.

"From here the road just goes away from where we want to be. The Gable's property is just a few hundred yards further. Let's go back and I'll walk you out to the ridgeline."

We turned around and went back about a quarter of a mile. Peter parked the car and we got out. It was trying to snow again. There was a path that led through the trees and underbrush away from the road.

"This will take us to the highest accessible part of the ridgeline. The path parallels the property line of the Acorn's land just to the left of us. I think they have about five or ten acres."

The ground we were on was fairly level. We walked about two hundred yards and came to a sign that had 'Danger Steep Drop-off Ahead' written on it.

"That's for the hikers and cross country skiers that aren't familiar with the area. The ridge is just ahead."

We weaved around a final few pines and the path turned sharply left. It had no choice.   There was nothing but air straight ahead.   Someone had placed a number of large boulders directly in line of the path as an attempt to stop anyone who might not have seen the warning sign.   If a person missed the sign and the rocks, there was nothing but about a hundred or so yards of fresh mountain air between him and the rocky ground below.

"Nice view," Peter said.   "Right below here is where the second girl was found. Be careful how close to the edge you get, I don't trust the ground. There is a rocky point just down there a little bit." Peter pointed down the path. "I'll show it to you as we go by. A couple of hikers saw her body from it."

The path sloped gradually downward as we walked along winding along the ridgeline. I stayed to the left side of the path. We quickly came to a point on the ridgeline where two immense rock features shot out over the open air below.

"I wouldn't suggest we go out on them now, with the snow and all, but when it's warmer and dry a lot of hikers come up here and sit out on the rock."

"I don't think you'd catch me out on that even in the summer," I remarked.

"It's quite secure. This formation has been looked at by some engineers, or maybe scientists. Anyway, they say it would take a major earthquake to shake them loose. At least that's what someone told me."

We continued walking down the trail. The terrain to our left opened up into a meadow and I could see the Acorn's house not far away. There was no sign of life.

"Right below here another of the girls was discovered. It's just as steep here but the fall is much less." Peter stated.

I peered over the edge getting as close as I dared. "Far enough," I commented.   "Although I can't imagine how anyone would accidently walk off the edge."

We headed back up the path towards the car. I was feeling more convinced that these incidents were not all accidents. The snow had tapered off but the wind was still gusty and it felt like a significant storm was just around the corner.

We drove down to an area in between the Acorn's property and the Hamilton's. There was no path to walk on but the ground was fairly flat with a few trees in between the road and the ridge.

"Who owns this land?" I asked.

"I'm not sure. A lot of this land belongs to the government now as part of the National Forest. But this could be private."

It seemed like the road where we stopped was further from the ridgeline than before as we walked for some time to get to it. We turned right going back up hill a ways and stopped at a place where the trail narrowed significantly between a ten or fifteen foot high natural rock wall and the precipice to our left.

Peter looked at the map again. "I think last year's body was found somewhere right below where we are now."

"At least I can see how someone could fall off here, the path is quite narrow. You can even see where the ground has given way right there." I pointed to a place on the ridge where it looked like nearly a foot of soil had broken off at some point and fallen below.

We eventually headed back down the path. The slope was very gradual now and the ridge bent around to the left a little. The cold wind was now in our face.

"Hope it's not far to go," I said. "This wind is freezing."

"Not too far. Both of the next two locations are by the Hamilton's property line."

We walked for about fifteen minutes when Peter stopped and again studied the map. He looked around as if to get his bearings and walked closer to the ledge than I would have thought was safe. "I think this is where the Hamilton's daughter went off. The drop off here is about seventy yards. As I mentioned before, the further down the trail we go the drop off gets considerably less and the slope starts to flatten out."

We walked about another five minutes and stopped. "We are on the Hamilton's property now. This is the end of the rock face," Peter explained. "You can see how the ground starts going out away from the trail a little further down. Not the straight drop off that you have here. Right below us is where the last girl was found. Actually, we may have missed one." He started studying the map again.

"That's all right. This has been good to see. Let's head back to the car before we freeze."

We started back up the path to the edge of the Hamilton's property and then cut diagonally across the field towards the car.

Chapter 12

Once in the car, I asked Peter if he had talked to the Hamilton's in his investigation. He said he hadn't so I asked if we could stop just to follow up on a few thoughts that I had. He thought it would be alright and we drove down to their house. Even though it was early afternoon, there was little sunlight and we could see the lights were on in the house. There was also an old station wagon in the driveway.

"Looks like they're home," I said as I got out of the car.

We both walked up to the front door. Before we could ring the bell, the door opened and the man I saw at the pharmacy stepped out.

"May I help you gentlemen?" he asked. He looked at me. "Didn't I see you last night," he paused for a second as if in thought, "at the pharmacy?"

"Yes you did," I said, "but that's not why we are here."

"Mr. Hamilton, I'm Deputy Peter Blanco with the Lincoln County Sheriff's department. Could we come in to talk to you for a moment?"

For a second a startled look came over his face then he recovered. The back of my neck started giving me signals. I've known for a long time that when the authorities show up unannounced it is normal for people to react, but I've also learned to pay attention to the back of my neck.

"Why?" he asked, "What's going on?"

"Mr. Hamilton," I interjected, "you are not under

investigation or anything like that, we are just looking into something and you might be able to help us."

"Well, okay, but we'll need to stay in the den. Mother's not doing too well."

He opened the door wider and let us in. He immediately directed us off to the left where there was a small sitting room with some books in a built-in bookshelf, a desk with a computer, a couple chairs, lamps and some houseplants.

"What can I do for you gentlemen?" He asked again when we were all seated. He took the chair behind the desk.

Per our discussion in the car, I took the lead. "Mr. Hamilton, we are looking into the disappearance of Melissa Ribbons. You may have heard of her. She is the young lady..."

"I read about her in the paper," Mr. Hamilton said interrupting me. "It's a shame, but I don't know anything about her. If that's why you came you just wasted your gas."

"Benny," the woman's voice came from some other part of the house, "who are you talking to?"

"Just some visitors, Prissy, don't mind us they are just leaving." Then turning to us, "you'd better go," Benny instructed. "I told you she is not doing well."

"Is that your mother, Mr. Hamilton?" I asked, knowing it probably wasn't but I didn't want to be chased out the door.

"Of course not, my mother's been dead for a dozen years. Oh, excuse me I did refer to her as Mother, didn't I? That's an old habit of mine. That's my wife."

A stocky woman appeared at the door to the room. "Oh, hello," she said. She did look frazzled. Her grey hair was a mess. She didn't appear to have on any makeup and she was dressed in a bathrobe with some old slippers. She had what I thought was a dress folded over her right arm.

"Can I get you gentleman some tea or hot chocolate?"

"No need dear, these men were just leaving," he said and stood up to further make his point. "Please go back to what you were doing, Prissy."

"Yes, I will," she answered. "I was just ironing."

"Thank you dear," Benny remarked as his wife turned and walked away.

"Jackie died seven years ago. It's hard on Mother this time of year." We moved back into the hall and towards the door. We passed a small open coat closet. "She still keeps a lot of Jackie's old things, her skies and boots and jackets."

I glanced in as we passed. The small closet was crammed with coats, jackets, boots, and on the shelf above a wad of gloves and hats. I could only see the bottom portion of the skies mixed in with the boots. As we walked out the front door I suddenly got a strong feeling I was missing something but I didn't know what.

"Something is not right in that house." I said as we got back in the car.

"You can say that again; both of them were weird. They gave me the shivers. Did you ever see Misery, the movie? That old woman reminded me of that crazy lady."

"That's not what I mean." But he didn't respond as he steered the car back down to the main road and back towards Ruidoso.

We discussed stopping by the apartments in Nocelo but I decided to skip it as I did not think looking at an empty apartment would serve any purpose at this time. I had to do some thinking, something was nagging at my mind and I had to get my brain around it.

It was just as well as Peter received a call on his cell just as we hit Ruidoso city limits. "They want me to come back to the headquarters for a briefing. I guess they expect some bad weather later on this evening and have a contingency operations plan they want to brief to everyone."

"I thought you were on leave for a couple of days."

"I am, but this overrides that. I will likely just be placed on reserve call up in case they need more people tonight. We go through this a number of times every winter. It's fairly routine. Sometimes we have to close down roads and help with emergency evacuations of stranded motorists, but nothing more exciting than that. These storms usually blow through in a few days." He sounded like he was actually happy to be called back in to work.

I had him drop me off at a Denny's a few blocks from the hotel. I needed to think and did not want any distractions. I ordered a cup of coffee and went back over the known facts behind each of the victims. In my mind now they were victims, something had happened to them beyond coincidental accidents.

First there was the very similar age and appearance of each of the girls. Second you had same manner of deaths, severe falls that probably killed them, or at the least led to their freezing to death. Thirdly you had the timing of each disappearance, all of them happening in the weeks preceding Christmas. Finally you had the discovery locations. Each one was aligned with the others along the bottom of a ridgeline that spanned less than two miles.

We also knew some things that didn't happen. The girls weren't shot or strangled and other than the damage that was likely caused by the falls, had no other signs of abuse. None of them showed any signs of rape. There had been months between disappearance and recovery on all but the Hamilton girl, but as they were covered and packed in snow, each was fairly well preserved.

But there was also a lot that we didn't know. We did not know motive and we did not have any suspects. The perpetrator didn't even have to live in the Ruidoso area. It could be any of the thousands of tourists that return to the area each year over the holidays. None of the victims' lives were connected in any way other than coming and dying here in the cold snowy slopes of south central New Mexico.

I knew nothing of the families of any of the victims other than Melissa. I didn't know if any of the victims had been heavy into the drug scene, had alcohol problems, boyfriend troubles or had other emotional issues that may have resulted in their deaths being suicide. Besides the difficulty in doing so, there had not been a good reason for anyone to try to prove that any of the incidents were suicide. What value would there have been in that? A death in the family is hard enough to handle, why throw more kindling on the fires of guilt and sadness. It would have served no purpose.

Yet if one or more of the deaths were a result of suicide, my entire theory would take a serious hit. If one was to throw out the first incident and Melissa, who could still be alive out there somewhere, four in a row is a lot stronger than say two in the last four years. But I didn't believe any had been a suicide.

No matter whom our killer was or where he or she or they were from, they would have first had to have spotted the victim. Easy to do. They then would have to catch or trap the victim. Not so easy, but not too hard. They would have to keep and conceal the victim for an unknown amount of time. Not too hard if you had the privacy but not something you could do in a hotel. Finally, they would have to dispose of the victim. A little harder to do without being seen, but then I didn't see anyone on my trek through the ridgeline trail earlier in the day.

The weak links would be in the capture and the disposal. It was too late to do anything about the capture but something could be done about the disposal. If the victims were being dropped or pushed over the ridge, then a thorough surveillance of the trail could catch the bad guy in the act.

My adrenalin was picking up. For the first time since getting the phone call from John Ribbons, I had come up with something specific to do that I thought had a good chance of succeeding.

The killer had a routine. Serial killers almost always do. They don't like changing their routine and there was no reason to think our killer would change his at this point. He would return to the ridge to dispose of Melissa. I was confident of it and I had a gut feeling he would do so by Christmas. Today was the twentieth.

There were two big problems I had to consider. First, did our bad guy kill his victims before transporting them to the ridge or did he let the fall do it for him. I could argue this debate for either side so I decided to ignore it and just hope he kept them alive. The second problem was simply whether or not I could drum up any support for my theory and garner the assistance of the sheriff's department or maybe the FBI, if they would accept my argument of this being a kidnapping. I needed manpower to make the surveillance work, a lot of it.

I took out my cell phone to call Peter and get his thoughts on the chances of the sheriff's office helping out in a surveillance.   I normally keep my phone on silent and looking at it saw I had missed two calls.   I keep it on silent for obvious reasons.   One, I don't like most phone calls, and two, I don't want my phone to make a noise at times when I'm trying not to be noticed.

The first message was from my neighbor.   They are nice people and their kids takes care of my dog when I'm away.   With the snow and ice on the roads in Clovis, someone ran into my mail box.   Please call when I get a chance.   Maybe tomorrow.

The second was from Kristi.   She just wanted to say hi and to confirm our dinner plans.   I called her back and confirmed.   She said there was a reporter from the paper hanging around for a couple of hours over lunch.   She suggested we just meet at the restaurant rather than the Mescalero Café.   I agreed and told her I was looking forward to it. I was.

I called Peter and told him my thoughts on a surveillance of the ridgeline trail.   He liked the idea but said it might be hard to persuade the Sheriff.   It would consume a lot of manpower.   There was no way anything could be done tonight but he said he would discuss the idea with the chief deputy and call me back.   He didn't seem all that optimistic.

My next call was to Gene Jordain, an old FBI contact I had worked with on a few occasions.   After a few minutes of small talk, I explained to him my predicament.   I reassured him that my call was informal, just a chat between old friends, but I needed his advice on whether the FBI might be interested in getting involved in this.   If not what would have to be done to get them interested.

"This is a bad time of year to try to generate any kind of interest," Gene answered. "Everyone is trying to get things wrapped up or at least put on hold until after the holidays. Besides it is very unlikely that the FBI would do anything without a formal request from the local authorities. Doesn't sound like you have that. I guess if you got Congress excited or maybe the governor and they put some pressure on us it would cause some enthusiasm."

"You know that's a non-starter." I said. "I figured the odds were poor. You are not aware of something like this happening before somewhere, are you?"

"Not off the top of my head. Nothing like what you described going on out there. I do think you have a good theory. Have any of the people living up and around the trail you referred to seen anything in the past? Strange cars, lights, people that kind of stuff?"

"If they have, no one has documented it. Like I said the authorities here have treated the incidents as accidents. Some of them have started to change their minds but not enough of them. My main concern is to do something for my client, if it is not already too late. I don't have any more time to debate the old cases."

"I understand," Gene stated. "Let me talk to one of our profilers and see what she comes up with. We can get the newspaper stories off the web. I'll try and call you back tonight or tomorrow."

We said our good-byes. I looked outside. The snow was falling again and the wind seemed to have gotten stronger. I figured that I had about ninety minutes of daylight left and maybe that much time before the roads got too treacherous to travel. I left Denny's and quickly hiked back to my hotel. It took me a good twenty minutes.

Chapter 13

I skipped going to my room and instead jumped into my car and headed out of town in the direction of Ski Apache. I had no problem remembering the route Peter took earlier today. I drove past the Hamilton's and turned onto the Acorn's driveway. There was a light on in the house.

I got out of the car and walked towards the front door. The snow was still falling but not as heavily as when I left town. One side wall of the small front porch had a plaque that said Jim and Betty's House. As I rang the doorbell I glanced through the narrow door length window and briefly saw the top of what appeared to be a woman's head. The hair was blond. She was sitting on a couch facing away from me. Although I wanted to get excited, I knew the chances of the blond being Melissa were slim.

The reason I only caught a quick glimpse of the blond was now answering the door. He was a big guy, taking up most of the door frame when he opened the door. He had stepped out of a room inside the house as the door bell rang and had blocked my view as he approached the door. Now he was blocking it again.

He looked at me and then out past me, I guess looking to see if I was alone. "What do you need?" He asked.

"I'm Jim West," I said holding out my hand. He didn't take it. "I am helping the police in their search for a missing woman, Melissa Ribbons, you may have read about her disappearance in the newspaper."

"I haven't spent much time here in the last few weeks. So I don't think I can be any help to you." He said and started closing the door.

I put up my hand as much to get his attention as to slow the progress of the door. "Please, hear me out for a second. This current disappearance may be related to the past disappearances of four young women, all of whom were found dead at the bottom of the cliff in your back yard."

"Wait a second," he said angrily, "are you trying to imply that I have anything to do with any of those girls."

"No, not at all," I said trying to mollify him. "I just wanted to see if you could remember anything out of the ordinary that may have happened around your property during the month of December in any of the past five years."

"I don't remember anything out of the ordinary ever happening here. Sorry, but if you want to talk more, I suggest you bring the police with you next time." He again started closing the door.

"One last thing," I said in a hurry. "How about your wife, could I just ask her?"

"There's no one here but me."

He could probably tell by my expression that I knew he was lying. If he was bright enough he realized that I knew that he knew that I knew that he was lying. Or something like that and was now trying to decide whether to just close the door in my face or first kick me down his driveway and then come back and close the door.

Luckily for me a woman's voice broke the silence.

"Jimmy, who is it?"

"It's nobody Carol."

Just then Carol's head popped around the hulk standing

menacingly in front of me. It wasn't Melissa. This lady was closer to thirty than twenty and looked a lot rougher around the edges than I hoped Melissa would ever look.

"Ma'am, I'm looking into the disappearance of a young woman, Melissa Ribbons. Her disappearance may be related to a number of other young women who turned up missing in December of each year. I was just wondering if either of you have noticed anything strange around here recently or in any of the Decembers past."

Carol looked at me and then at Jimmy. "I wouldn't know." She then looked back at me with a hint of a smile.

"Get lost," the big guy barked and shut the door a little more forcefully than he needed to.

I went back to my car. Although they weren't any help, I had figured out that Carol wasn't Betty and Jimmy's main concern was getting rid of me so he could get back to Carol. I doubted if Carol knew anything, she probably didn't even live close by. I would have to come back with Peter and do a real interview with Jim and Betty. My gut told me though that he wasn't involved with Melissa but maybe he had seen something in the past and simply wasn't in the mood to discuss anything with me.

I followed the same route that Peter had taken earlier in the day making a u-turn when the road turned away from the ridgeline. I hadn't intended to stop but there was a land rover and a pickup truck parked near the spot where we had parked earlier.

The weather was not conducive to hiking or otherwise having a good time so I wondered what anyone was doing parked out here. There was no one in either vehicle.

I parked and got out. The trail was still visible but there were a few inches of fresh snow on it. I could see the footprints of four people. I followed the footprints. As I rounded the first bend, I heard voices and stopped.

"It's all there, count it if you want, but I've never stiffed you," shouted an angry male voice.

"I know it man, it's just good business, you know?" responded a second.

"Yeah, we bring you some good stuff. You can cut it and make a fortune this time of year. We can't cut the money, what we get is all there is. It's good business to count the money," said a third voice.

I took a step closer and peered thru some underbrush. There were four men huddled together, undoubtedly meeting here in seclusion to conduct a transaction involving some illegal drug. Besides having no authority to do anything, I was unarmed and alone. I backtracked to my car, copied down the two license plates and drove away. I kept an eye on my rearview mirror but I didn't think they saw me.

My next stop was the Hamilton's. As I walked up to the door, I heard a car. I turned and saw the Land Rover drive by. I couldn't tell if either person in the Land Rover looked over at me or my car. The snow was starting to come down a little harder.

I rang the doorbell and this time the door was opened by Mrs. Hamilton. She was dressed the same and still look disheveled.

"Hello," she said with a smile, "how are you?" Before I could answer she continued.   "Weren't you here this morning? Where's your friend? Oh, I think we are going to get a nice snowfall this evening. Please come in, I'm just icing a cake."

She stepped back to let me in but as she did so Mr.

Hamilton appeared in the doorway. "Who are you talking to Prissy?" On seeing me he frowned. "I thought we finished our conversation this morning."

He was considerably older than me and didn't pose a physical threat but still his voice sounded threatening. More than it should have.

"I thought of a couple more questions and felt that maybe the two of you could help me with them. "

"Prissy, go back in the kitchen and finish what you were doing." He said it in a way that did not sound like a command but rather like he was coaxing her.

"Oh, okay honey. I don't want the icing to get hard." She waddled away.

"What did she say to you?"

"Nothing but hello and it looked like it was going to snow. Look, Mr. Hamilton, a young girl is missing and all I am trying to do is locate her." He stared at me but said nothing. "I think Melissa's disappearance may be connected to the last four girls that died up here of falls and exposure. All four disappeared in December and were found at the bottom of the rock face, a good part of which is at the end of your backyard. I just need to know if you or Mrs. Hamilton had seen anything unusual out along the trail this past week or in any of the last four Decembers?"

He stared at me. His face was flushed, for a second I thought he was having heart issues. "Go away, mister. If you need to interview me you'd better bring the police with you." He closed the door.

I walked back to my car. I found it strange that neither Acorn nor Hamilton appeared to have any interest in helping to find a missing girl. I could partially understand Acorn's feeling if he was in the middle of an adulterous fling when I rang the door bell. Hamilton on the other hand was harder to rationalize. He had lost a daughter and certainly could empathize with what the parents must be going through. Yet he was very direct in his unwillingness to do anything to help my finding Melissa. Maybe it simply hit too close to home for him.

It was starting to get dark as I backed out of the Hamilton's driveway. I drove about four hundred yards down the road and stopped. I could see a path leading from the road towards where the ridgeline would be, except the ridgeline I knew stopped further up the trail. Peter and I had not come down this far. I decided to take a quick look to see if the trail came to or past this point.

Just like the top of the road where Peter and I first walked out to the trail, this path weaved through and around a terrain filled with Pinon trees, other larger pines and a lot of underbrush. The ground was not flat as it dipped and rose with every dozen or so steps I took. In just a few minutes I ran into the trail. I turned right and followed the trail up a slight incline for about a hundred yards. There was no cliff to my left but as I went further up the trail the slope of the drop off did steepen. Yet even as I stopped the incline didn't look that bad. If it wasn't for the snow and probable icy patches underneath the snow, one could hike down it or climb it. I could see where the rock face began a hundred or so yards ahead of me. I felt fairly certain that anyone trying to get to this trail at this time of year could only do it by walking from the road that ran in front of the two houses. It might be possible to join the trail further down and walk up it, but a surveillance of the trail would pick the person up as they crossed the path I just walked from the road.

It was getting darker fast so I turned back to head down the trail and to my car. I had only taken one or two steps when something buzzed by the back of my neck right below my right ear. I realized what it was as soon as I heard the explosion of a rifle shot from somewhere above me. I instinctively jumped behind some boulders. Give my instincts an A for speed but an F for direction. My leap took me to the edge of the slope and my momentum and the slick snow took me over. At first I was just sliding and bouncing off the ground and small bushes, cursing myself for not being able to stop.

Then things quickly got worse. I slid off a small cliff, dropped about six feet and landed on a fallen tree trunk. It hurt and I grabbed for a branch to stop my slide. I managed to get a hold on some small branches but they were too small and too rotted to do any good. My slide continued and as I hit a rough patch of ground my slide turned into a tumble. Again I went into the air and then everything went dark.

Chapter 14

Lightning flashed in my mind somewhere. I realized I was outside and it was cold but where? I had been this cold before, but that wasn't now was it? I tried to wrestle the fog out of my head but I couldn't. Where was I this cold before? I knew I was dreaming but it came without effort. I finally remembered where I was so cold. It must have been twenty years ago. I was on a stake out. The DEA and the local sheriff's office shared the lead on the case. But it was our information and I got to tag along. Besides it was a small group of airmen that were smuggling the heroin in from Asia. We were all there to observe the sale and then make the bust. My role was to mostly stay out of the way and I was given the ignoble task of staying secluded near the small boat dock in the vast back yard of the lake house. My post was about two hundred yards from the house in which the transfer was supposed to take place. The dock belonged to the house along with about five acres of land that sat on the edge of Choke Canyon Reservoir, in south central Texas.

Our intelligence was that the heroin was going to be delivered by car to the home by two to three individuals and sold to a similar three to four members of the Mexican Mafia. Everything was supposed to take place at the house. My job was to notify the main team, which was everyone else, if anyone tried to come or leave by boat on the lake. No one was expected to do so.

It was a dark November evening, around seven. The sky was overcast and the temperature in the high fifties. I could see the lights of the house just fine and a couple lights on backyard poles provided sufficient lighting to see objects and movement in the immediate backyard. Closer to the boat dock it was a lot darker.

The plan didn't go as expected. No surprise as plans rarely do but this time it nearly got me killed. The house was vacant when we got there. About twenty minutes later a car and a van pulled up and eight men and two big dogs got out. The Mexican Mafia had shown up in force. Three went into the house and the other five started a cursory sweep of the area with the two dogs. The dogs were Rottweiler's.

At first I thought I would be okay. The men didn't seem to have any real interest in doing much walking. They posed no threat to the main part of the team as they were parked behind the house across the street. I would have been alright too, except a deer had come down to the lake shore for a drink about twenty yards from me. I didn't see it but the dogs did. They both started howling and their walkers let them off the leashes. I didn't know if the men could see the deer or if they just wanted to let their dogs have some fun.

The dogs never had a chance of catching the deer. It simply had too much of a head start. I could hear them barking as they ran after the deer in the darkness. The barking finally stopped. The two handlers kept walking and getting closer to me. One of them started whistling to call the dogs back.

The two men were still a good fifty yards from me when I heard the dogs again. They were trotting back into view immediately to my left. I knew the men couldn't see me and thought everything was going to be fine when one of the dogs stopped. It looked in my directions and growled. Then the other one started growling. At first the dogs stood still but then one of them started walking at a diagonal to me but looking in my direction as he did.

"Que pasa, Tino? Mas venado?" asked one of the walkers. I saw him remove a handgun from his belt. His partner did the same and I could tell the other men back in the yard now were taking some interest in what was going on.

I had good cover as long as I stayed low but my only escape was backwards into the water. I didn't think the dogs had actually seen me but rather had caught my scent. They were still a bit cautious as they knew what they smelled was human but were unsure exactly where I was.

I really only had one option, the lake. I was armed but shooting these men would be tantamount to murder at this point as the crime we had come to act on had not yet happened. Besides, there was just one of me, five of them and two nasty dogs. I had to swallow my pride, back up quietly in a crouch and slither into the water.

The dogs caught sight of me at the water's edge and charged. Luckily the lake bed fell off to about six feet deep just a few meters from shore. The dogs entered the lake but quickly turned back when their feet no longer touched the ground.

I was swimming away from shore looking back with just the top half of my head out of water. The dogs were still barking but fortunately had no interest in coming back into the lake. A flashlight popped on and started scanning across the water, then another came on.

I had sensed the cold right away but did not pay attention to it. My thoughts were just set on escaping. Now the cold was gaining priority. I had to make a decision soon, where to swim. Two possibilities were out. There was no returning to the shore I just left and it would be impossible for me to swim the mile and a half across the lake. Looking back at the house from about fifty yards out, I could see movement by the boats. I also saw flashlights patrolling the shoreline. All five men had come down to the lake.

If I swam to my left I could come ashore anywhere but I would have to make my way across a lot of land to get to the rest of the team. I decided it would be safer to swim to my right. It was a longer swim as I would have to swim around the point of land sticking out into the lake and to a point where I could get out of the water in the backyard of the house across the street. I didn't think I would have to go too far once I rounded the point, I just had to get to friendly land.

I started swimming sidestroke keeping as much of me as I could underwater and yet still keep an eye on the men onshore. I heard the sound of a small motor start up, cough a couple of times and stop. I start swimming with more urgency. The motor started up again and died again. No gas or bad gas I thought. A flashlight beam shot out in my direction and I ducked underwater swimming as far as I could before I had to come up for air. The lights were now checking a different part of the lake.

I kept swimming occasionally changing strokes. The cold started to affect me. I rounded the point close to shore and was tempted to get out and walk the rest of the way. I decided against it. I figured I had already swum about three hundred yards, what was one more hundred?

I went about a hundred yards further when I realized my teeth were chattering and my fingers were numb. I must have been swimming those last few minutes in a daze. I turned towards shore in something close to a panic. I kept telling myself I have to get out of the water. I have to get out of the water. I have to get out of the water.

I sat up in a start, a sudden pain ripped through my side. Water didn't surround me. I was in snow. My head was pounding and just like that old memory of the lake, my teeth were chattering and my fingers were numb. For that matter, so were my toes. Struggling to my feet I felt woozy and leaned against a tree. I coughed and spit snow, blood and dirt out of my mouth.

The snow was coming down harder now and it was dark. I knew I had fallen but I didn't know exactly where I had fallen from. The back of my head had a nasty bump and my ribs on my left side hurt like hell.

I had to start moving and going down slope seemed the easiest way to go. The terrain was rough and I wasn't making much progress. Not liking my odds, I called out for help. No answer. I kept walking. I hit smooth ground for a while and then I was back in the underbrush, trees, rocks and ravines. I had to back track a couple of times. I was getting tired and light headed again. I pushed against my ribs. The pain was sharp but it brought some clarity back to my mind. I wasn't sure how much further I could go.

Suddenly I saw movement. Instinctively I froze. Being shot at does that, but I quickly realized that it was irrational to think anyone had followed me for this long in this darkness. Besides the person that came into view looked female and was jogging in what looked like a white jogging suit and a darker stocking cap.

"Hey!" I shouted. She kept running, crossing barely fifteen yards in front of me.

"Help, please." She slowed, looked at me and started jogging off.

"I won't hurt you, I'm lost." She kept running. I started running after her. I couldn't run fast, the conditions were terrible and I hurt. She disappeared behind some trees and I thought I lost her, but when I rounded them there she was again. I could barely see her in the dark.

My only thought at this point was that she, at least, knew where she was going. I would follow her until I couldn't go on. I tried calling to her again but it took up too much breath. I slipped once and fell. When I looked up she had stopped. When I got up she started jogging again. We slowly ran on. I just focused on her and moved my feet. At some point my mind clicked into semi-consciousness as everything came sharply back into focus when I literally ran into a parked car. It knocked me off my feet and I sat there in the snow under the lights of the parking lot to the Backwoods Bar. I looked around for the female jogger but she was gone.

Chapter 15

"Mister, are you okay?" A man asked. I looked up. He was standing on the front porch of the bar smoking a cigarette. "Are you okay? I mean you just ran out of the woods and right into Steve's car."

I started to stand up and slipped back to the ground. I rolled over moaning and tried again. Suddenly I felt a pair of hands grab me under my arms and lift me to my feet. It was the big guy who had been our waiter for lunch.

"You better get inside, you look like you are about to freeze to death." He half carried me into the bar. A handful of people were at the front door watching. He looked at them as we passed, "I told you the food was good here, look how determined this man was to come back after experiencing one of my gourmet lunches." He chuckled at his own joke.

He chased away two guys sitting at a table closest to the fireplace and helped me sit down. "Stella, bring this man a coffee and some Jack." Then turning back to me, "Seriously, are you okay?"

"I think so, but I might not be if I didn't somehow find your place. Say, the guy that first saw me out in your parking lot, did he say if there was a woman with me?"

"No, that was old Ralph, he just came in and said a man needed some help out in the parking lot. What in the world were you doing out there? You look half frozen."

I looked around. There was no woman dressed in white in the bar. However, there was someone I recognized who was approaching me, the young waitress with the tattoo from the Mescalero Cafe. I couldn't remember her name.

"Mister West, have you been in another fight? I'm sorry to say this but you look a mess."

"I feel like a mess but no, I have not been in a fight."

A red haired woman wearing jeans and a red sweatshirt delivered the coffee and shot of Jack Daniels.

"Just the coffee," I said, taking off my gloves. Despite the gloves my hands were partially numb.

"Drink the Jack," the redhead instructed, "then you can sip on the coffee, it's hot."

I didn't feel like arguing so I drank the Jack. It took me a second to get a good grip on the glass. I'm mainly a beer drinker so it gave me a little jolt.

"More?" The redhead asked.

"No thanks."

She walked back towards the bar.

"Mister West, let me help you take off that jacket, it's starting to drip water everywhere," offered Miss Tatoo. Before I could answer my young friend leaned over and grabbed the zipper on my jacket. She was wearing a heavy green sweater that was cut low in the front. Despite our age difference and my damaged condition, I was mesmerized by that tattoo. I imagine it did more to get my blood flowing than the Jack.

"I can do that," I said and brushed her hands away. I stood up and the dizziness set back in. I leaned against the chair.

"Let me help you," she insisted but my head cleared and I finished unzipping my jacket. I did let her help me with the sleeves. She took the coat over to the wall and hung it on one of a dozen coat hooks on the wall.

"How did you end up in the parking lot?" She asked, sitting herself in the chair opposite me.

"I'm not too sure myself."

"Where's your car?"

"Back by the Hamilton's place, I don't know the street name or address."

"Never heard of them," she responded. "Your shirt is all wet. Is that from the snow or sweat? By the way, aren't you supposed to on a date with Kristi about now?"

I looked at my watch. It was broken and full of melting ice.

"It's five 'til seven," she said. "You'd better call her."

"My cell phone is in my car, is there a phone here I can use?"

"Let me get mine," she said and got up and went back into the room where the pool tables were. It was a few minutes before she got back. I studied the inside of the bar again. There were about a dozen customers, but no lady in white. I was beginning to wonder if I hallucinated the whole thing. A head injury could do that and the lump on my head was large and painful.

The coffee cup was warm and my hands started thawing out. The smells coming from the grill were beginning to make me hungry. At least my hunger was no hallucination.

"She's coming here." My tattooed caretaker had returned without my seeing her. "She said you both could just eat here, but I told her she needed to first get you home and cleaned up. Anyway Kristi is on her way, so you better get cleaned up the best you can if you have any desire at all to impress her. The restroom is over there." She pointed to the far end of the bar.

I gave her a half-assed salute and proceeded to the restroom. My legs were stiff and sore but I managed. For the second time in as many days I was shocked at my own appearance when I looked into a mirror. I was going to have to stay away from mirrors for the rest of my stay in Ruidoso. This didn't happen to me in Clovis.

The damage done to my face the day before didn't look any worse for wear but now the right side of my face had long diagonal scratches that stretched from my chin to my right ear. They didn't appear deep and there wasn't much blood. My right cheek was also covered with dirt. During my fall I must have scraped that side of my face against something, probably the ground. My hair was a matted mess and my nose and ears were a shiny red. I was a pitiful sight.

I washed up the best I could in the sink and dried off with the rough paper towels. I combed my hair. Raising both hands to the top of my head made my ribs ache. I didn't think they were broken. In the end I was presentable, but barely so.

I walked back and sat down at the table. The redhead was sitting there with my tattooed friend. Both ladies looked at me and smiled. The redhead got up and left.

"That's a little better. I've arranged with Stella for you and Kristi to have the table over there in the corner. It's a little more private than this table."

"You didn't need to, but thanks." I had already resigned myself that I would be here for a while. I had no car, and besides I needed something to eat. "Is the weather safe enough for Kristi to be driving?"

"Sure she has a four wheel drive. She'll be fine."

"What are you doing here?" I asked.

"It's my off night and I'm here with my boyfriend. He's playing pool with his buddies right now. They take their pool playing seriously." She rolled her eyes. Obviously she didn't.

Stella came over and refilled my coffee. "The table is ready for you if you want to go over there now." She nodded in the direction of the table. The globe candle was already lit.

"Thanks, but I'll wait here for Kristi. It's closer to the door."

A jukebox, or whatever they call them these days, started up in the pool room. I didn't recognize the song. For some reason, my tattooed guardian stayed with me and gave me an in depth rundown on the limited menu until Kristi showed up.

When she walked thru the door the overhead lighting struck her and I instantly remembered why I agreed to dinner tonight. She looked great. Snowflakes sat briefly still frozen in her hair and on her shoulders. Our eyes met and she smiled. I did too. She walked over and I stood up.

"Are you going to live long enough to have this old town in your rearview mirror?" She asked shaking her head. "You messed up what was left of your face. Ellen thanks for babysitting my date until I could get here."

"No problem," Ellen replied. "But be easy on him tonight, I think he has a few new injuries other than his face." She excused herself and went into the pool room.

"They have a table for us back in the corner," I said pointing to the table.

"Do you feel up to eating?"

"I do now. I'm starving."

We walked back to the table and sat down.

"First," she said as she handed me a small shopping bag, "put these on and let your feet thaw out. Ellen said to bring you new socks and shoes. These slippers will have to do. There is a Target close to my place so I just grabbed these."

My first reaction was to say something like you shouldn't have, but my feet were still cold and wet. "Thanks, I owe you."

"How are you feeling? I understand they found you lying down in the parking lot?"

"I fell down. Actually I ran into a car and fell down. I don't want to bore you with the details, but I'm not even sure what happened to me this evening."

"Ellen also told me on the phone that you didn't drive here, how did you get here in the dark, in this weather?"

I didn't think I wanted to rehash the evening's events and was granted a temporary reprieve by Stella showing up and asking us if we were ready to order. Kristi apparently had eaten here before.

"Let me have a chili cheeseburger with fries," she said with a grin. Then looking at me, "they are famous for their chili cheeseburger."

"Sure, I'll have the same. To drink?" I asked.

"Dos Equis," Kristi said without hesitating. I nodded the same and the redhead went back towards the bar.

"So how has your day been?" I asked.

"Uneventful, until Ellen's phone call. You still haven't told me what happened."

I did not want to get into it all until I had it sorted out myself, but looking into her eyes I knew she wasn't going to let me off the hook.

"Can I summarize?' I asked. "I'd really rather talk more

about most anything else."

"I guess so," she said with a fake frown.

"I went back up to the area Deputy Blanco and I had been to earlier today. We walked along the trail that follows the ridgeline below which all the victims' bodies were discovered. While we up there we talked briefly to the Hamilton's but the Acorn's weren't home."

"I take it they are the people that live up there along the trail."

"That's right. I wanted to go back up and to see if the Acorn's were home and to talk to the Hamilton's again. After brief conversations with both of them, I walked back out to the trail. While I was there someone took a shot at me and missed but in my effort to find some cover I stupidly went over the edge and started tumbling and sliding down a fairly steep incline. Luckily I was below the part of the trail where it just drops off. I don't know how far I slid, rolled, tumbled and fell. The next thing I knew I came to with a mouthful of snow and knot on the back of my head. "

She instinctively got up and came around to feel the back of my head. "Wow, you do have a goose egg there. We should get you to the hospital. You may have a concussion."

"I'm fine, let's worry about going to the hospital after dinner."

"Is that how you scraped you face, too?"

"I'm not exactly sure when that happened, but it probably happened at the same time, as did the bruise to my ribs."

"Considering you could have frozen to death out there, you are lucky. How did you ever find your way here in the dark?"

"That's the funny part and don't think I'm crazy. I was

wandering around lost when all of a sudden a young female jogger goes right by me. She doesn't say a thing and won't answer my calling to her. She looks back at me but just keeps running. I figured she knew where she was going so I followed her. Luckily she wasn't running fast. She stayed about fifteen yards ahead of me no matter how slow or fast I was running. I was tiring and thought I'd never make it to where she was running. All of a sudden I was in the parking lot and wham there was a car."

"Believe me no one jogs out here in the dark and more so not in a snow storm in the dark, especially some gal by herself."

"I know that. None of it makes sense to me either. The blow to the head must have caused me to hallucinate the whole thing but it seemed awful real to me at the time. And dream or not, she got me here to this place. I never would have found it on my own."

"Did you recognize this jogger?"

"No, although she could have been any of the victims. She was youngish, blond hair, wearing a white jogging suit and a dark stocking cap. But it was dark and there was a lot of snow falling. I never had a very good view of her."

"Was it Melissa? She is the one you are here to find. Do you think your mind was just playing tricks on you?"

"It's a safe bet my mind was playing tricks on me. I was a little woozy. But I never thought it was Melissa."

"Do you know who it was that tried to shoot you?"

"No, I never saw anyone. I just felt a buzz go by my neck and almost simultaneously heard the shot. It was a rifle shot."

"Are you going to tell the police?"

"Yes, I'm not sure what they can do about it. But I'll tell

them in case the next time the guy doesn't miss."

Our dinner arrived and our conversation became intermittent as we focused our attention on trying to eat the enormous pile of hamburger and chili that Stella had placed in front of both of us. The chili was spicy and delicious. We both finished our first bottles of Dos Equis long before we made a serious dent in our dinner and ordered a second round.

"Do you think you are any closer to finding out what happened to Melissa?"   Kristi asked me as we were finally close to finishing our meals.

"I feel like I am, Kristi. There is nothing concrete I can put my fingers on, but I sense that some pieces of the puzzle have been given to me and I just need to figure out what they are and how they fit into the puzzle."

"In the movies, Jim, the detectives gut feelings are normally right. Maybe yours will be too."

"We'll see. Something needs to break soon." I knew I would have to face John in another day or two. More importantly, if Melissa was still alive, I didn't think she had more than a day or two left.

"That was good," I declared when we were finished eating, "too much, but good. I'm really sorry I messed up our plans though and to drag you out here to rescue me."

"I enjoyed my dinner. I like to come out here now and then. And you didn't ruin any plan I had, because it was just to have dinner with you.   Where we ate never mattered."

"Would you like dessert or anything else?"

"No thanks, I'm stuffed. Besides, I want to take you by the clinic to have that head of yours checked out."

"I don't think that is really necessary," I responded

standing up. Betraying me my ribs shot a quick jolt of pain through my side as I stood. I didn't think I grimaced but she saw something.

"And they need to x-ray your ribs to make sure nothing is broken."

I acquiesced. I didn't have enough energy to argue and I was starting to think something might be broken. Rather than put my wet socks and shoes back on I just kept the slippers on. We put on our jackets and headed outside.

"Brrr!" Kristi exclaimed. The snow was falling harder now but the temperature was cold enough that nothing was melting. Someone was keeping the sidewalk swept or shoveled and there was less than a half inch of fresh snow on it. I only had to wade through the deeper snow in my slippers for the last few feet. Once in the Jeep the dry snow was easy to brush off.

I made a half hearted offer to scrape the windows but fortunately the wipers knocked most of the snow off the windshield. We sat in the Jeep with the defroster blasting away for a few minutes to clean off the rest before we left.

"Do you know how long you were unconscious," she asked. When I said I didn't, she continued. "It is definitely a good thing you came to when you did because an unconscious person doesn't last long out here."

"Luckily I had a recurring dream, almost a nightmare, that I have had a few times in the past that usually wakes me up at the same point in the dream every time."

"What is your dream about, or is it personal? I don't mean to pry."

"It's not personal. I don't mind talking about it, but it will likely just bore you."

"Try me," she said with that grin again.

She looked very pretty sitting there with the lights of the restaurant penetrating through the snow and windshield to cast a glow upon her face. I leaned over and kissed her. She kissed me back.

We drove slowly back to Ruidoso. The roads were bad but passable. Upon further prompting, I gave her the abbreviated version of my dream and answered her questions. Yes, the bust still took place and was successful. Yes, getting out of the water and into the cool air made me even colder. Yes, everyone got a good laugh out of my watery retreat. Yes, I would do it again if all the circumstances were the same.

Chapter 16

"Weren't you here yesterday?" asked the chubby reception nurse at the hospital's small emergency room. With her glasses, white hair and rosy cheeks she could have doubled as Santa's wife. I didn't remember seeing her yesterday. "You wouldn't think a grown man would be out getting himself banged up every day. I hope you weren't fighting again."

I wasn't sure if she was kidding or not. "No, this time I just slipped and fell."

"Well, have a seat and the doctor will be with you shortly."

There was no one else in the waiting area and another nurse appeared within a few minutes to take me to see the doctor. This nurse was barely five feet tall and probably weighed less than a hundred pounds. Probably one of the elves, I thought, half expecting the doc to be old St Nick himself.

I told Kristi she was welcome to come and she did.

"Beats sitting out here alone," she remarked. "Plus you may need someone to hold your hand."

As I was walking out of the waiting room, the reception nurse noticed my slippers and looked at Kristi. "Did he dress himself this morning?"

As we entered the hallway Kristi leaned over to me, "That was rude. I don't think they should be allowed to talk like that."

"I'm sure that's just her sense of humor. She's probably having a slow, boring evening and we just livened it up a little. It didn't bother me."

To my chagrin the doctor didn't have the smallest resemblance to Santa. Although I had to admit I'm not sure if they have a Santa in India, or if they do, what he would look like. Dr. Singh Patwaanish seemed very competent to me, though, and that was all that really mattered. After taking x-rays, blood pressure readings, temperature, looking at my eyes, ears, nose and throat, poking and prodding my head and ribs, he declared I was fit to go home. No broken bones, no concussion, and he even liked my slippers.

We left the hospital almost to the hour after we arrived.

"One more trip here and they will give me my own parking spot." I said as we climbed into her Jeep.

"Hopefully you won't need to come back. You just need some sleep."

"Your place or mine?" I said as I slid closer. Our lips met and lingered.

After a few minutes she pulled away. "Not tonight, Jim. I want to, but I need another day or two."

"Sure, I understand," of course I didn't, but I never did understand women. "Let me buy you dinner tomorrow night at the steakhouse where we were supposed to meet tonight. No strings."

"It's a date," she said with that grin again. "And don't try to stand me up. You know I'll just drive out into the country and find you like I did tonight."

Kristi dropped me off at the entrance to the Brown Bear Inn. The sign next door was flashing twenty seven degrees through the lightly falling snow. I walked into the motel shoes and socks in hand. Rose was behind the counter.

"Working late tonight, Rose? I thought you had the morning shift."

"Mac has the flu today and Gene was already tied up. So I get to pull an all-dayer. I don't mind. I get overtime or double time off. I can use both during the holidays. Say, you just missed Roger with the local paper. He's been camped out here or across the street for most of the day."

I instinctively looked back towards the café.

"He's not there now. He had some meeting at his kid's school. Parent teacher conference or something like that. It looks like the snow is slowing down some. I don't think it will be as bad as everyone thought. You never know though. Say, what happened to your shoes?"

"They got a little wet." I was tempted not to say anything. The way Rose's conversation was rambling on I imagined she was on her twelfth cup of coffee and would probably just keep talking whether I answered or not.

"Easy to do out there in this kind of weather. Yep, easy to do." The phone rang and I made my escape.

My room was too warm so I turned down the thermostat and started throwing my clothes into a pile on the floor when I noticed the message light on the room phone was flashing. I picked up the receiver, dialed the required extension and listened to my message.

"Hey, I was just calling to see if you were feeling better. Hope you are. I have an appointment this afternoon for a massage. Why don't you join me? We could have loads of fun. Give me a call." It was Marge, she went on to leave a number but I wasn't interested.

I thought about calling John but his number was on my cell and it was still in my car. I also considered calling a cab and going to get my car but decided it could wait until morning.

The pain in my ribs flared up again as I took my jeans off. I wondered if the doc could have missed something on the x-rays. I stood there in the nude and looked at myself in the mirror. My side was black and blue from just above my waistline to my armpit. There was bruising where the bullet had grazed my hip yesterday and my face looked a mess. It was no wonder that Kristi wasn't ready to take me home. If she was waiting for me to heal, I was going to have a long wait. Tomorrow, I absolutely had to take better care of myself.

I walked into the shower and turned the water on hot. It felt good. I stood there and focused again on the reason I had come to Ruidoso. I needed to get the surveillance set up as soon as possible. My gut told me Melissa was still alive but it also told me she wouldn't be for long. I didn't have anything concrete to support my theory but until today the snowfall since Melissa's disappearance had been light. If the killer followed his or her same pattern Melissa would be pushed off the ridge. If he had done so already, Peter or I would likely have spotted her body. I knew we missed a lot of territory but we saw a lot too. Besides it would make sense for the killer to want to wait for a heavy snowfall to help hide the body. I didn't like the fact that it was snowing today but the snowfall had been predicted for a couple of days and was supposed to last through the next two days. If I was the killer, I would wait until the snow had started falling and then make my move once I was sure it was going to continue. That would mean sometime in the next forty eight hours.

That, of course, was also dependent upon the killer

having a logical approach to all this which was unlikely. This killer had to have a few screws loose.

I didn't think the druggies had anything to do with Melissa and Acorn was more interested in keeping his lady friend a secret than anything else. I didn't feel comfortable about the Hamilton's but other than their being a little weird I didn't have anything specific to link them with the case either.

The key would be the surveillance. If we could surreptitiously observe the trail I was confident we could catch the killer.

I turned the water off and dried myself with the not so soft white towels. The white became blotched with red and I discovered the wound on my hip was oozing blood. I found the gauze and tape the hospital had given me the night before and covered the wound.

The temperature in the bedroom had already dropped a few degrees, so I readjusted the thermostat, grabbed the television remote and jumped into bed. The ten o'clock news had just started. After a few minutes covering the several traffic accidents in the area caused by the snowstorm, the news focused in on the events I was involved with yesterday. First they announced that in addition to the drugs they found in the warehouse, the police had found evidence linking the gang to the murder of a drifter earlier this year. They then announce that Deputy Joe Maldonado was expected to make a full recovery but that Teddy Munoz' condition was still listed as critical. Finally, the announcer said that confidential sources had claimed that the Sheriff's office was investigating possible links that the gang may have had with the missing girl, Melissa Ribbons.

I shook my head. No way. There was no obvious link to her and a close-in source had denied it. Plus, Teddy's denial to me was too quick and straightforward. I didn't think he was lying. Looking deeper into Teddy's gang to find Melissa would just be a waste of time, but it would be something I would have to overcome if I expected any cooperation from the Sheriff's office.

I tossed and turned a lot that night. The interest in Munoz and his gang with regards to Melissa's disappearance was annoying but it wasn't the major factor for my lack of sleep. I kept thinking there was something I was overlooking, something that should have been obvious.

When I did sleep I kept having strange dreams. I dreamt I was swimming in snow. I dreamt I was being buried in snow and I dreamt I was jogging after my female ghost in the white jogging suit and red hat.

The red hat! I sat up in bed. It was six thirty in the morning and still dark outside. That was what was bothering me, the red stocking cap, ski cap or whatever you call it in the Hamilton's closet was a match for the one worn by one of the victims in a picture I had seen. It was the picture of the girl with the two sisters who became a victim two or three years ago. It wasn't just red, it had a small yellow star or something like a star embroidered on it.

If the hat was just plain red or even red with a yellow logo or a yellow stripe, then it could be just a coincidence. But I didn't think it was. I would have to look at the picture again and compare it to the hat at the Hamilton's. I was almost sure the yellow patch was an aftermarket add-on, of just what I didn't know.

I didn't get a close look at it at the Hamilton's. It was just there in the closet as we walked by. That was what had bothered me. I made my mind focus on those few moments. I could see it plainly. A red stocking cap flopped up on the shelf. Where the fold of the cap faced the door I could see something yellow, just a small piece of yellow in an otherwise solid red cap.

What else was in the closet? Boots, girl's boots. Why would they be there? If the family wanted to hang onto their child's things, would you keep them in the hall closet?

I knew I was getting ahead of myself. Follow your hunches but don't think you have the final solution until you have sufficient evidence. That's what I use to teach my rookies and I needed to remember it now.

I got up and shaved the best I could, trying to miss all the cuts on my face. I put on my khaki trousers. I needed to keep these clean or I would be doing laundry tonight. I finished getting dressed and went out to find some coffee.

Chapter 17

The lobby was empty but I could hear a male voice coming from the office behind the counter area. He must have been on the phone as he was having a conversation with someone but I could only hear his voice. I walked out of the hotel into the cold, cloudy and windy morning with my heavy jacket in hand. I promptly put it on and made a bee line to the Mescalero Café. It looked empty but its lights were on. I was hoping this early on a Saturday morning I could get in, eat and get out without running into the press or Marge. I wasn't sure which would be worse.

"Good morning, Jim." Daisy welcomed me as I entered. "Glad to see you up and active this early on a Saturday."

"Thanks, Daisy, can I just talk you out of a big cup of coffee and one of those cinnamon rolls you gave Peter the other day?" I asked as I sat down at a table next to the counter.

"Certainly," she replied, "what did you do to your face? The last time I saw you I thought you had half a face that wasn't cut up. Today your whole face looks like a tomcat got mad at it."

"I'm just going for the rugged look."

"Ragged is more like it. Has Kristi seen you like this?"

"Yes," I replied. "If I promise not to scratch up my face any more, will you get me some coffee?"

"Oh, sorry, I do get distracted. One coffee and cinnamon

roll coming up."

She hustled back to the kitchen area. I got the impression no one else was working yet. The road outside was already active with weekend skiers driving in to hit the slopes.

The weather didn't appear to me to be very good for skiing. The wind chill and low visibility might even result in the ski area being closed. About four inches of new snow had fallen over the night in town. I thought more had been forecasted but I imagined the higher altitudes had already received more.

Daisy brought the coffee and cinnamon roll.

"Any luck in your search?" She asked.

"Hard to say but I hope so. Daisy, I thought from what people were saying that this was supposed to be a bigger snowstorm than this. Have you heard an updated forecast?"

"This morning on the radio they said we should continue to get snow through tomorrow night. Supposedly we could receive a total of a foot of snow here and more up around the ski area. They need it, as of yesterday only about half the slopes were open. But you know it's not always the amount of snow that's significant, it's the wind. That wind makes visibility horrible when it's snowing and can cause snow drifts. I know because my neighbor's garage is situated in such a way that the snow seems to always pile up right in front of the garage door. He hates it. I can just back out of mine and I see him over there shoveling away."

"Daisy there are taxis here in Ruidoso aren't there?"

"Sure, but you have to call them. They don't just roam the streets. I thought you had a car."

"I do but I left it up on the mountain yesterday."

"You want me to get Larry to drive you up there?"

"Maybe later Daisy if it wouldn't be too much of a

problem. First thing I need to do today is talk again with the police and the sheriff's office."

Daisy went to get the coffee pot to refill my cup as I attacked the cinnamon roll that covered my entire small plate. I made quick work of it and then took my time with the second cup of coffee. I knew there would be someone at the police station around the clock but I wanted to make sure the day shift was in.

I paid for my breakfast and told Daisy I would be in touch. I walked down to the police station and got there a few minutes before eight. The clouds looked menacing but no snow was falling yet.

I entered the police station. The young officer Sergeant Morrison had referred to as Buddy was behind the front desk.

"Good morning, Mr. West. You are up early today. What can we do for you?"

"Good morning to you Buddy, is Sergeant Morrison in today?

"No, in fact I believe he is taking his wife and kids over to Roswell today to do some Christmas shopping. They may have already left. Do you need me to call him for you?"

I would have liked to have gotten Rick's support before contacting the Sheriff's office. "Not now, by any chance is the Chief in?"

"I don't think so but let me buzz Ms. Cane. I saw her this morning."

"No need to buzz me Buddy, I'm right here."

We both looked up. Ms. Sharon Cane, Captain Marshall's secretary had just entered the front desk reception area from the hallway. She was dressed casually in jeans and a red cardigan sweater.

"Ms. Cane," Buddy asked, "is the Captain in this morning?"

"No, I just came in to finish up a few letters he wants to get out first thing Monday morning. Do you all need him?"

"Not enough to call him into the office," I responded. "I just wanted to bounce something off either Sergeant Morrison or Captain Marshall. It's something I need to address with the Sheriff's office. I just thought if my ideas made sense to them it might give me some leverage with the Sheriff."

Just then the door to the street opened and an elderly couple came in and started complaining to Buddy about someone stealing the Christmas nativity scene from their front yard.

"Mr. West, can you step back into the hallway for a second?" I did as Sharon Cane asked. "If this has to do with your theories on the girls' deaths being related, I can tell you that Rick and the Captain had a long discussion about that yesterday afternoon. I believe they both tend to agree with your assessment. I may be talking out of school so keep this to yourself but they both think you are on the right track. I know Captain Marshall has already had a phone conversation with Sheriff Mendez."

"I'm glad to hear that."

"I don't know how the Sheriff responded or if he has passed on any instructions to his deputies."

"That's okay. I can find that out, I'll call over there in a few minutes. My main concern is how much time Melissa has left."

"Do you think she could still be alive?"

"I don't know, but if she is we need to find her soon."

"I wish there was something we could do, Jim, but the

Sheriff's office has the lead in this. If you come across any reason to believe Melissa may be somewhere in the city, let the Captain or Rick know immediately. I'm sure the Captain has already offered the department's support to the Sheriff."

I thanked her and told her to pass along my thanks to the Captain. I left the building without talking to Buddy who was still talking to the couple about the stolen nativity scene.

Outside the snow and wind had picked up again. It didn't look like it was going to be a nice day. I walked back to my hotel room to make the call to the Deputy Peter Blanco.

He answered on the second ring.

"Hey, Peter, this is Jim, how are you doing this morning?"

"A little tired but fine. I was on reserve last night and had to respond to a truck going off the road around midnight. No one was hurt so as soon as I got out there they sent me home. What's up?"

"Did you get a chance to talk to the Chief Deputy about the surveillance I discussed with you yesterday?"

"No. Sorry, Jim, I'll talk to him this morning and call you back."

"Please do so, Peter. I understand that the Sheriff may have had a phone call yesterday from Captain Marshall supporting our position. The Sheriff, in turn, may have already called his Chief Deputy. Hopefully, they are already looking for ways to further investigate Melissa's disappearance."

"Well, no one's talked to me yet."

I knew what Peter meant. If the Sheriff was anxious enough to give the case a high priority someone in his chain of command would have already called him.

"Just let me know when you do hear something. By the way, I may have a lead for you in a drug operation you may have going on in your backyard. My note's in my car, though, so I'll have to get it to you the next time we talk."

"Looking forward to it, I'll call you back this morning."

"One other thing, Peter, when we were in the Hamilton's home did you see a red ski hat in the hall closet?"

"No, why?"

"It looked just like the hat owned by one of the victims. I know there must be a million red hats out there, but this one had something yellow embroidered on it. It's worth checking out, that's all." I knew I sounded like I was grasping at straws and maybe I was.

"I don't know Jim, doesn't sound like much of a lead."

After I hung up, I sat in the chair thinking. I didn't tell Peter about my being shot at simply because I wanted to do that in person. I knew there was very little anyone could do about it as I didn't see the shooter and only had a general idea from where the shot had been fired. The fact that I wasn't hit by the bullet would make the incident almost insignificant. But it wasn't to me. The fact that someone would try to shoot me meant that I was perceived by someone as a threat, or at least a serious nuisance.

There were a number of possibilities. Although unlikely, it could have just been a kook. But I knew crazy people who just shoot at other people are very rare. It could have been one of the four individuals involved in the drug transaction. They could have seen me but I doubted it. It could have been one of Teddy's gang, or even a family member. But that meant they would have had to have been following me and I never noticed anyone on my tail. It could also have been someone involved in the abduction of Melissa. A possibility that I was hoping was the right one as it supported my other theories.

The phone rang and I picked it up thinking it was Peter.

"Hello, Jim?" I almost didn't recognize the voice. It was Martha Ribbons. I hadn't talked to her in years.

"Yes, that's me."

"Jim, it's Martha. John and I will be arriving there tomorrow. Jim, have you learned anything?" Her voice was cracking. It had none of the false bravado of her husband's.

"Martha, all I can say is I'm more optimistic today than I was two days ago. I don't mean to give you any false hopes, but I don't want you to lose all hope either. With any luck by tomorrow I'll have a more definitive answer for you. How are you arriving?"

It took her a few seconds to answer. I knew she was trying to maintain her composure. "We will be flying into El Paso and driving a rental car from there. John thinks we will get there around noon."

"When you arrive give me a call on my cell or here at the hotel. I'll be close by but I still have a few things to do."

Martha was unwilling to hang up. "What has happened to her, Jim? Where is she?"

"I don't know but I am working on a couple of theories. I'm not giving up and neither should you." I hated myself for sounding too optimistic and leading her on. Even if my theory was correct and Melissa was alive, we didn't know where she was and until we did, we couldn't protect her if the killer decided to get rid of her.

"Thank you Jim, thank you very much."

"I'll see you tomorrow Martha." I hung up, staring out the window. What was I going to say to them when I did see them?

I left the hotel feeling a lot more depressed than I had since my arrival. I needed the support of the Sheriff's office to mount an effective surveillance, but they seemed to be in no hurry and time was running out.

Chapter 18

I had to get my car and as it was next to the trail I planned to just hang around the trail all day. That might discourage anyone from taking Melissa up there, but with the trail being so long the killer could come, dump the body and leave and it would be likely that I would never see them.

My luck wasn't going to get any better soon. As I stood there in front of the hotel an old pickup truck pulled into the parking lot of the bank next to me. A man jumped out and went up to the ATM window. Although I had only seen him that once, I was sure the man was Pico, one of the two men who assaulted Deputy Joe Maldonado.

Without my cell phone, I couldn't simply call the police while I stood there and watched him. I didn't want to run back into the hotel as he might leave while I was gone. I needed to walk past him and get the attention of the security guard inside the bank. I knew most banks employed security personnel and was hoping this one did.

He was busy at the ATM as I passed him. No one else seemed to be in the parked vehicle. I was just getting to the bank door when I saw Pico turn around and start walking slowly back towards his truck while counting the cash that was dispensed to him.

I opened the bank door searching for anyone in a security uniform. I saw him, an overweight man sitting in a chair at the far corner of the bank. I whistled and shouted "Hey!"

Everyone looked towards me, including the guard. I motioned with my hands for him to come and turned around and went back outside without waiting for a response.

Pico was standing at the pickup truck with the driver door open. He was still counting, or perhaps recounting his money. I didn't want him to leave. I also didn't want him to get into the truck. I figured I only had to stall him for a few seconds. I pulled a dollar out of my money clip and dropped it next to me.

"Hey, sir, is this yours?"

He looked at me and saw the bill I was pointing at on the ground. I knew the ATM's didn't dispense dollar bills but I was hoping he didn't notice that it was only a dollar bill.

Pico started walking towards me and I leaned over and picked up the money. I held my hand out towards him with the bill folded. He came up to me and took the cash without even looking at it. I guessed he didn't care if it was his money or not. He was more than happy to take it.

He placed the dollar bill in the same jeans pocket that he had stashed the rest of his cash when he approached me. He mumbled something like "thanks," and turned back to his truck.

When his back was facing me, I turned and looked back at the bank door. Still no guard but someone, probably an employee was watching me out the glass door. I motioned again that I wanted someone outside, hoping the person watching me would relay the message to the guard.

I turned back to Pico.

"What no reward?"

Pico turned his head and grinned at my joke. He slowed but didn't stop and now he was almost back to his car.

"Pico," he turned again and looked at me. I called him by name because I wanted to make sure it was him before I did anything more. It was him.

"Do I know you?" His eyes were more alert now. He glanced around.

"We met just once, a while back." I started walking slowly in his direction. "That was a hundred dollar bill I gave you. Was it really yours?"

He just stared at me. You could almost see his mind trying to figure out who I was. He made no move to check out the bill.

"Get lost," he snarled and turned to get into his truck.

I glanced back at the bank door. The door was open part way and I could see a small crowd staring out at us. No one was moving. I knew if I wanted to prevent Pico from leaving, I had to make the first move. And I didn't want Pico to get away.

I leapt and kicked the open door as hard as I could. I caught him leaning into the vehicle. The frame of the door smashed against his left leg and shoulder. As the door bounced off him, I grabbed his left arm and yanked him out of the pickup.

He yelled in pain and I spun him around in an attempt to control him from behind, but he was faster than I was and desperate to escape. Rather than allow me to get a grip on him from behind he kept spinning and slashed at me with a switchblade as we came back face to face. The blade of his knife tore at my jacket but failed to reach skin. I stepped backwards and the knife slashed through the air inches from my face.

Although I was taller and heavier than Pico, it was obvious to me now that he was an experienced street fighter.

The speed of his counter attack with the knife that seemed to come out of nowhere was all the evidence I needed to realize that any mistake I made now could be fatal.

I moved to my right away from Pico's knife hand. He circled to his right keeping me in front of him. I could see over his shoulder the security guard barrel out of the bank, nothing like a fight in the parking lot to get his attention.

I stepped back to stay out of Pico's range and to give the guard time to reach us. Pico saw my retreat as a loss of will and charged in with his knife, this time thrusting the knife straight at my stomach as he got in range. I countered slamming my fist down on his knife hand as the blade tore into my jacket. I felt the blade pierce my skin but I knew he barely wounded me.

The force of my blow momentarily stunned the nerves in his hand and knocked his hand away from the knife entangled in my jacket. I stepped back to get leverage and kicked through his right knee. Pico screamed in pain and collapsed on the pavement.

As he fell, I saw the security guard standing in a crouch position, weapon drawn and aimed at me. He was shouting and looked nervous. I only now heard him.

"Let me see your hands! Get on the ground! Show me your hands!"

I slowly raised my hands. I didn't want to startle him.

"It's okay, now. I'm the good guy. Remember I was the one who came in and called for help."

He kept staring at me. Despite the cold temperature, I could see the sweat on his brow. I noticed he was staring at my chest or stomach which spooked me at first as I knew basic law enforcement weapons training teaches you to shoot there, but as I looked down I realized he was probably fascinated by the knife that appeared to be sticking straight out of my stomach.

"You can see my hands," I reassured him. "I'm on your side but you need to keep a close eye on this guy." I pointed down towards Pico. "He is one of the men who tried to kill Deputy Maldonado. Have someone call the police while you watch him. I'll stay right here."

"The police have already been called," a lady in a burgundy business suit remarked from the bank door. I saw a couple of other people were also standing outside the bank door now.

The security guard shifted the aim of his revolver to Pico.

A siren from a police car erupted just a few blocks away.

"Jim! Jim! Are you all right?"

I looked around and saw Daisy and Ellen running across the street towards me from the Mescalero Café. Their arrival made me smile and helped calm down my agitated state. On the other hand, the knife sticking out from my jacket seemed to have the opposite effect on them.

"Kenny," Daisy addressed the security guard as an old acquaintance, "Mr. West needs an ambulance."

"No, I'm fine. I think the knife barely cut me." I looked at the security guard. "Can I remove the knife?"

The guard hesitated too long and became the focus of Daisy's wrath.

"For God's sake Kenny, Jim is working with the police. He is one of the good guys. Let him take out the damn knife or I will."

Before I could do anything, however, the Ruidoso police arrived and two young officers jumped out with weapons in hand.

"What's going on?" The driver asked.

"These two men were fighting," responded the security guard.

"Officer," I interjected, "this man is one of the men who assaulted and left Deputy Joe Maldonado to die the day before yesterday. I believe there is a warrant out for his arrest. I just tried to keep him here until you could arrive. My name is Jim West. Sergeant Rick Morrison can vouch for me."

"We can, too." Ellen remarked.

"Okay, you can go into the bank and have a seat. We'll need a statement from you once we verify who this man is." As the driver was talking the other officer had returned to his car and started talking on the radio. Another police sedan pulled up and two more police officers piled out.

"Let's go inside and sit down," Daisy said as she took my arm to give me some support.

"I'm fine Daisy. Let me give this knife to the police officer first." I pulled the knife out of my jacket. It was caught on some material but ultimately came out without too much further ripping. I held the knife out in the palm of my hand to the driver of the first police vehicle. He, in turn, instructed one of the recent arrivals to take it from me and bag it as evidence. The other police officer that arrived in the second police car was busy handcuffing Pico.

Once I was relieved of the knife, I walked into the bank with Daisy and Ellen. The crowd at the front door parted in front of us as though we were contagious.

I walked over sat down on an overstuffed chair. Daisy and Ellen sat on the adjacent couch.

"Are you sure the knife didn't cut you?" Ellen asked.

"It cut me but the blade did a lot more damage to my jacket than it did to me."

I looked down at my jacket. I had only brought two jackets with me and now they were both ruined.

"I may need to buy another jacket, it seems as though I've been going through them rather quickly."

An ambulance siren wailed as it approached the bank. I looked around. All the tellers and customers were either looking outside or at us.

"Why were you fighting that man?"

"Ellen, didn't you hear Jim outside. That other man was one of the men that tried to kill that Deputy. Why Jim was just making a citizen's arrest."

I smiled at Daisy's faith in me but before I could comment the bank door opened and the police officer who was the driver of the first police car that arrived and who appeared to be in charge walked in with one of the medics from the ambulance. They walked right up to us.

"Mr. West, we appreciate you detaining Fontana for us. I corroborated your story with the station and partly with the manager here at the bank. She is mad at the guard for not being quicker in responding to you. How did you recognize Fontana?"

"I only know him as Pico. I was there when Pico and another man assaulted Deputy Maldonado. I saw him then. I knew there was an outstanding warrant for him and I just didn't want him to get away."

I turned to the medic. "How bad is his knee?"

"Bad."

"Good, he's a very bad dude."

"How are you? Someone said you might have been stabbed. There was blood on the knife."

"That is my blood," I admitted.

"Can I see?"

I turned away from the gawkers in the bank so I was facing the wall and unzipped my jacket and pulled up my shirt exposing the gash at my waistline. There was already a lot of blood on my shirt and pants.

The medic opened the small case he had been carrying, tore open some packaging I couldn't see and pulled out some moist towelettes which he used to clean the surface area of my stab wound.

I noticed that Daisy was politely looking away while Ellen was staring with interest at the process.

"It doesn't look that deep so you should be okay. Have you had a tetanus shot recently?"

"Not that long ago."

"I recommend you get some stitches to keep it closed, but for now I'll just apply some antiseptic on it and put a few butterfly bandages on it to help keep it closed and stop the bleeding. Do you want to ride back to the hospital with us?"

"No, I'll check in later." The last place I wanted to be going was back to the hospital. Twice in two days was enough. No reason to make it three for three.

"I'll need to get a statement from you later today," remarked the officer. "Nothing fancy, just how you saw and recognized Fontana and how he attacked you. Can you come by the station after you have your wound looked at?"

"Sure, not a problem." I could fill him in with the minor point that I may have provoked the attack later. Additionally, I didn't think I would have time to spare to make the statement for another day or two. I needed to get back up on the ridge and get some help from the Sheriff's office as soon as possible.

After a few minutes of small talk the officer left. Daisy was still there but Ellen had walked off with the young medic.

"Daisy, do you think Larry might be able to drive me out to get my car?"

"I don't know why not. We best get Larry now, though, he'll want to be back for the lunch crowd."

"That's perfect. We can probably leave Ellen here, she looks preoccupied."

Daisy just smiled as we walked out of the bank toward the Café.

The snow was falling harder now and visibility was down to a half a mile or so. I imagined at the higher elevations it was worse.

"I hope Larry doesn't mind driving in this stuff."

"This is nothing. You should have been here in ninety-eight. It snowed like this for days. We had a couple of feet of snow on the ground. But, you know, we never had to close the café a day because of the weather."

As we entered the café, Larry yelled at Daisy from behind the counter. "Anybody die?"

"Nope, not this time," answered Daisy.

"Where's Ellen?"

"I think she may be finding herself a new boyfriend."

"God, how many does she need?" Larry retorted.

"Larry, do you mind driving Jim out to get his car?"

"No, where is it?"

"It's near the turn off to Ski Apache." I really didn't know how else to describe the location.

Larry looked at his watch. There were no customers in the café.

"We'll need to go soon so I can get back before the lunch hours."

"I'm ready when you are." I was used to the term lunch

hour. I guess as the proprietor of a restaurant there were lunch hours.

He looked at me, "Do you want a different jacket?"

I looked down. My jacket was a mess. "My other one looks worse than this."

Daisy came over and took another look at me. I thought she was studying the jacket.

"Larry, he might be able to fit in your old navy blue ski jacket. I think his shoulders won't be too big and he'll have excess room in the belly." She winked at me, smiling at herself.

"Very funny, Daisy," Larry responded, "but you are welcome to my blue jacket. I haven't worn it in a long time."

"No, I'm fine with this jacket, holes and all."

"Don't be silly," Daisy remarked and headed off towards the back room. She returned a few seconds later carrying the blue jacket.

"Try it on," she instructed handing the jacket to me.

It was a good, heavy jacket, a little tight through the shoulders and chest but not a bad fit.

"You just wear that and give it back to Larry when you don't need it anymore."

There was no use arguing and my jacket did look a bit ridiculous torn up like it was.

"Okay," I said, "let's roll."

Larry led me out the back door to his car parked in the alley behind the café. He owned a dark green Volkswagon Passat that was about five years old. I climbed in the passenger side and after a few minutes of warming up the car and allowing the wipers time to brush off the snow, we drove down the narrow alley and out onto the road.

"If you just head towards Ski Apache, I'll be able to direct you once we are closer. Larry, I really appreciate this, saves me from having to call a cab."

"That's alright. Things were slow at the café."

"Is Kristi working today?"

"Yes, she should be in shortly. She has the lunch and early dinner shift today."

We rode along in silence until we reached the turn off for Ski Apache.

"Go ahead and take this," I said as we approached the intersection and as we turned, "and then you'll take your first left a little further up."

He did so and in a few minutes he had pulled next to my car. It was covered with about eight inches of snow.

"I have a brush that will make getting that snow off a lot easier, let me give you a hand." Larry offered it while opening his door.

"No that's alright. I know you need to get back and I have a scraper that also has a brush on it. Besides I want to walk out to the trail and look around for a second."

"You sure?" Larry asked.

"I am, thanks a lot for the lift."

I got out and Larry gunned the little Passat. It raced uphill through the snow. He made a u-turn at the Hamilton's driveway and sped on back by me on his way back to the café.

Chapter 19

I looked through the driver's side window of my car. Everything looked fine. I walked around the rear of the car and walked on towards the trail following the same approach I had taken yesterday. Today, though, I had to be more alert. The weather was bad and visibility wasn't anywhere close to what it had been the last couple of days. I didn't anticipate seeing anyone out on the trail but if there was anyone out there I needed to see them before they saw me.

Even though I had just walked this route less than twenty hours earlier, I had some trouble getting my bearings. The blowing snow and the fresh snow covering everything from shrubs to rocks made the entire area look different. I stopped and looked back at my car. I knew I had traveled perpendicular to my car yesterday and ensured my current route was the same. It seemed like it was and I didn't think anyone had moved my car, so I continued my hike towards the trail.

I was also concerned that I might not even see or recognize the trail and almost turned back. Finally I came to a point that I thought was the trail. I couldn't tell by looking down at the ground. Rather by looking right and left, I could see an open snow covered path that traveled for some distance.

I turned right with the goal of trying to find the place where I was the day before when someone took a shot at me.

I thought I would recognize it fairly easily and despite the new snow I did. I came upon the sight quicker than I expected but the large rock that I dove behind for cover and the scattered small shrubs I tried to grab on the way down were still discernable.

It was a little eerie standing there again and I quickly looked around to ensure no one was standing out there with a rifle. I saw no one. I was curious if there was any way that I could determine from where the shot had come. Recreating the scene from the day before, I imagined the flight of the bullet as it buzzed by my head. There was no way I could tell if the bullet was heading uphill or downhill but it seemed logical that the shooter would have been above me shooting down. The sound of the shot echoed through the hills but my impression yesterday was that it definitely came from an area back towards the road rather than from down the slope somewhere below me.

Studying the area that included part of the Hamilton's side yard and the open land next to it, there appeared to be several possibilities from where a person could seclude themselves and take a shot at me. As visibility was poor, there were probably more spots I couldn't see today. It didn't give me a warm feeling. I thought of reconnoitering a few probable locations but with all the fresh snow I decided it would be fruitless.

Despite the bad weather, I decided to walk further up the trail. I could only imagine the killer might be waiting for a day like this. Larry's jacket, along with my hat and gloves, gave me some comfort against the cold but I knew I couldn't be out too long.

I decided I could walk another twenty minutes up the trail and then do the forty minutes it would take me to get back to my car. I could then warm up for a while, call Peter, and then if necessary do the route again. I knew I would be missing over half the trail, but at the moment I didn't know what else to do.

I walked on and was clearly behind the Hamilton's house now. In the distance I could see the light on in the windows and thought I could see someone looking out at me. I kept moving and was just about to turn around when I saw two figures huddled on the path ahead of me.

One was much larger than the other. My adrenalin started up. Could it be a man and a woman? What in the world would they be doing out here in the cold. I quickened my pace and approached them. They didn't seem to notice me until I was right on top of them. When they did they both looked up at me startled.

It was Jim Acorn and he was with a different woman from the one I saw him with yesterday. This one had been crying. She instinctively raised a gloved hand to wipe her eyes.

"Excuse me,' I said, "I know it's not the best day for a stroll."

"You're the guy I saw yesterday, aren't you?" The way Acorn said it sounded almost friendly.

"Yes."

"Betty, this guy is investigating the disappearance of that young girl mentioned in the papers. Isn't that right?" He asked looking at me.

"Yes, I am."

"Betty, I told him I hadn't noticed anything peculiar around our house. Have you noticed anything?" I realized then that Jim and Betty were having a serious discussion and that Jim here wanted out of it any way he could. Even if it meant being nice to me, a guy he would have liked drop kicking out of his yard yesterday.   If Betty's arrival back home was earlier than he expected, she may have walked in on Jim and Carol doing things still illegal in seven states.

Betty looked at me with suspicion.

I didn't care if she thought I was part of some conspiracy with her husband, this was a good opportunity to ask her the questions I would have asked yesterday.

"It's true, Mrs. Acorn, I am here trying to find out what may have happened to Melissa Ribbons, the young lady who has disappeared. I asked your husband yesterday if he had seen anything suspicious in the last week back here along this trail.   I also asked him if he had noticed anything suspicious happening out here during late December in any of the last five years. He said he hadn't. How about you?"

"What do you mean suspicious?" She asked.

"Ma'am, there have been five young girls who disappeared in successive Decembers here in the Ruidoso area.   One in each of the last five years.   Four were subsequently found at the bottom of this cliff line months after their disappearance."   As I mentioned the cliff line I motioned my hands to indicate the one we were standing near. "Melissa is the fifth. My theory is simple. They either fell or were pushed off this cliff."

"You don't think they fell, do you?"

I shook my head.

"If my stupid husband here didn't have his head always stuck so far up his ass, or someone else's," she paused for a second to make a point, "he would have remembered that we had the same conversation around March of this year when they found that last girl. I told him at that time that I couldn't believe all those girls would just fall off the trail."

"Have you ever told anyone that?" I asked.

"No, maybe I should have."

"Did you ever see anything out of the ordinary out here?"

"No, actually I've never seen anything that you might call suspicious out here. I've seen hundreds of hikers and cross country skiers, but never anything out of the ordinary. I wish I could help you."

"Me, too. Can you both do me a favor, a simple one? While you are home these next few days can you spend a little extra time keeping an eye out your back window? If you see anything suspicious call the Sheriff's office."

"Sure," they both said.

"Thanks, I'd better head back."

"Good luck," Betty said as I turned.

Nice lady, too bad she was married to a loser. I walked back to the point where I thought was even with my car and turned toward the road. When I got close to the road I saw that I had walked down the trail a hundred yards past my car.

By now my car looked like a large pile of snow. I got my key into the door lock but struggled to get it to turn. It finally did and when I opened the door snow fell onto the driver seat from the roof. I brushed it out, jumped in and closed the door. It felt like I was on the inside of a refrigerator.

I put the key into the ignition and tried to start the car. All it did was groan. The battery, I thought. It had never given me any trouble but it was four years old and the engine was probably frozen. I turned the key again. The engine tried to turn over then died.

I looked over at my cell phone. It still had power and a signal. I could call a wrecker as I didn't want to bother Larry again. First I would call Peter. He might already be heading this way with reinforcements. I doubted it, but it still made sense to call him first. I dialed his number and his phone immediately went into voice mail. Probably in a meeting, I thought. I left a message letting him know where I was and that I would be waiting up here for a while for his call.

An idea came to me that this might be an excellent excuse to visit the Hamilton's again. I wanted to go there again but up until now could not think of a new reason to approach them. Surely they couldn't turn me away when I just needed help in calling a wrecker service.

I looked around inside the car to ensure there was nothing in it that I wanted to take with me. With the exception of my cell phone, which was now in my pocket, there wasn't. I got out, locked the car and began walking the few hundred yards to the Hamilton's residence.

The wind had started to pick up speed and was now blowing the snow across the road. The snow was striking my face with such velocity that I had to put my arm up to deflect the onslaught. It was a miserable day to be out. Hopefully the killer would be thinking the same thing.

My pace was slowed by the conditions which made getting to the house that much longer. By the time I arrived on their door step I figured no matter how much of a nuisance I was to them, they would have to take mercy on me and invite me in. If I had only known.

I stomped down on the porch to knock off most of the snow from my shoes and slacks and rang the doorbell. I saw some movement inside but no one came to the door. I resisted the urge to try to look through the translucent glass paneling that framed one side of the door and just waited. I was about to ring the doorbell again when the door opened.

Chapter 20

What happened next is still somewhat of a blur in my mind. Benny Hamilton opened the door and the first thing I noticed was his hand coming up and aiming a semi-automatic handgun at me. He fired it. The noise and the impact of the bullet caused me to step backwards stunned. My back foot slipped off the porch step and I fell backwards hitting my head on the sidewalk. Fortunately, my hat and the snow cushioned the impact.

I remember staring up at the white sky trying to regain my composure. I heard voices, one yelling at the other. The last thing I remember is someone grabbing me by my arms and trying to pick me up. My left shoulder erupted in intense pain as they did so and I must have blacked out.

When I started to regain consciousness, my first reaction was that I was in a hospital. A nurse was leaning over me cleaning and then bandaging my wound. She was singing something softly to herself. Then she was gone.

My mind finally started to focus and I realized I was in someone's bedroom. The Hamilton's house - that was where I was. I was lying on top of a bed. I tried to sit up but couldn't, something was restraining me. I was tied or strapped down. When I moved myself just slightly to look at my shoulder a sharp wave of pain shot through me. It hurt like hell but the pain also served to clear the cobwebs out of my mind.

The bedroom window's curtains were closed making the room dark, but enough daylight was getting through for me to make out the room. It looked like an unused spare bedroom, sparsely furnished and neat. A couple of paintings were on one wall. A dresser was on the other. From my angle it looked bare on top. The window was on the far wall. I had enough peripheral vision to know the door was behind me to my left. It was closed but I thought I could hear a lady singing softly to herself somewhere just outside the door.

I could move my legs and right arm. My left arm was free to move but more than the gentlest movement caused a lot of pain. My shirt was off and I could see that someone had done a pretty good job of bandaging and wrapping the bullet wound that was just under my left collarbone near my shoulder. I was restrained by something around my neck. I reached up and felt a metal band. It went all the way around my neck and was fastened to a chain that, in turn, was fastened to the floor, wall or perhaps just to the bed. The band had a screw that held it together at the base of my neck. The feel of the band made me think it was similar to the metal belts that you fasten the hoses of an automobile with, just larger.

The screw did not feel very big but the head of the screw was on the wrong side for me to effectively get to with my right hand. The more I tried to scrunch around to get a better grip on the screw only served to aggravate the bullet wound. I stopped after a few attempts.

I could turn my body slowly to the right but the chain on my collar was too short to get to a full ninety degree turn onto my side. I tried holding the collar still and turning my neck. I was having some success when I heard the door open.   Unfortunately, I now had myself out of position to look back to my left.

"I thought I heard you." It was Benny Hamilton.

I slowly rolled over onto my back.

"What in the hell is going on Hamilton? First you shoot me and then you apparently patch me up. Why any of this?"

"I didn't patch you up, that was my wife's doing. She used to be a nurse. I did watch her though. She did a pretty good job on you. The bullet went all the way through. She said it tore up a lot of muscle but only creased the bone."

"I'm relieved. Now why do you have me restrained in this bed?"

"Well it's kind of a long story. What was your name again?"

"Jim," I answered.

"Jim, I told you not to bother us again."

"I didn't come here to bother you this time, my car's battery is dead and I needed some help. You never even gave me a chance to explain."

"Well, Jim, that may or may not be true, but you did come back after I told you not to and you chose to come back on the one day of the year you shouldn't have. Your showing up like that really gave me no choice. I did warn you."

"You aren't making any sense, Hamilton, what do you have against today?"

"It's Jackie's birthday."

I looked at him for a minute not having any idea what the real significance of his comment could be. It took me a second to remember that Jackie was his dead daughter but that didn't really explain why he had shot me or why I was lying there a prisoner.

"I'm truly sorry about your daughter, Mr. Hamilton. I

know a little bit of the background but I didn't realize that today was her birthday. I still don't understand why that is a reason to shoot me."

"Like I said, Jim, you chose to come here today. That was your decision. That is why I shot you. The only reason you aren't dead is because my wife wants you to come to the birthday party. She has it in her mind that you are a friend of Jackie's. I tried to tell her you never even met Jackie but something you said yesterday made her think you are her friend."

I started to respond but didn't. Something about the tense he was using and the inference that I would be allowed to live at least through the birthday party, whenever that was, made me think about going in a different direction. Despite my intuition telling me I was on very thin ice, I had to ask.

"Will Jackie be at the party, Mr. Hamilton?"

He looked at me for a full thirty seconds before responding.

"If you ask me, no. But I'm not the one throwing the party. Just remember, Jim, there still are a lot of bullets left in that gun."

He got up and left the room. My hand instinctively went back to the screw at the base of my neck. Although I could reach the head of the screw I simply did not have the right angle to exert enough strength to budge it.

The door opened again. This time Mrs. Hamilton entered.

"Benny told me you were awake, Jim." He must have told her my name, too. "How is your shoulder?"

"Getting better. Thanks for patching me up Mrs. Hamilton."

"Please, call me Prissy, that's what all my friends call me.

It's short for Priscilla, but I've never been partial to my full name."

"Prissy, do you think you can take this thing off my neck. I really need to be getting home." I didn't know why she thought I was her friend but I was more than willing at this point to play along.

"With the accident you had, Jim, you shouldn't be going anywhere just yet. Besides, I know you won't want to miss Jackie's birthday party. Oh she is so pretty in her new dress."

"I am looking forward to the party, Prissy, and to seeing Jackie again." I watched her face intently as I could to see if I could glean any reaction. She seemed pleased by my comment but that was all.

"We still have a couple of hours, Jim, let me check your bandages and make sure everything is still okay." Rather than wait for a response from me, she sat down on the edge of the bed next to my head. For a brief second I contemplated trying to grab her with my right hand. I knew it would be a futile effort as all she would have to do was scream and Benny would be there with his gun.

As though she was reading my mind, she took hold of the back of my left arm just above the elbow and raised it a few inches. Pain pulsated through my body and I let out a loud gasp.

"Please don't make any sudden movements, Jim, and I'll do this as quickly as I can." She maintained a solid grip of my left arm as she peeled back a corner of the bandage with which she had dressed the wound. "Looks fine, now let me look at your back."

Luckily for me my raised arm allowed her to lean in close and inspect whatever bandaging there was on the back of my shoulder. She lowered my arm slowly.

"Not too bad, was it?   Just a little seepage, there is nothing to worry about. That will heal just fine." I thought I could hear some pride in her voice.

"I hope it will heal just fine. Will it be alright if I go home right after the party, Prissy?"

"Of course, Benny will give you and Jackie a ride home after the party?"

"I thought Jackie lived here."

"Oh no, not any more, she is a grown up now. She just comes home each year for her birthday."

The realization of what she had just said hit me like a rock.   All the pieces started falling in place. It had all been there before but they just didn't make sense. It was almost too obvious.   I started to say something to her when I noticed she had a syringe in her hand.

"Just something to fight infections and to help you rest for another couple of hours."

"No, don't do that." I protested. But there was very little I could do.

She inserted the syringe. "Now don't you worry Jim, we will get you up in plenty of time for the party."

I stared at her until she became blurry.

Unwillingly, I was back in my world of dreams. I was trying to climb out of a pit but things kept grabbing my legs and pulling me down. Struggling only made me tired so I just laid there in the pit. I seemed to know that I was dreaming but didn't care. My body and mind wanted to sleep.

Various visions crept in and out of my mind. I was back in Thailand as a young agent walking through a field in the dark. I had been warned about taking the short cut at night because of the snakes. But I was on an emotional high as we had just busted a major heroin smuggling outfit.   I had looked death in the face and survived.   At least that is how it seemed at the moment.   The fact that we had good resources, a lot of talent and an inside source didn't for the moment assuage my irrational sense of immortality.

I had the same decision to make that night as I had many times before walking home from the office to my bungalow. It was about a half mile walk and unless I was the Duty Agent and had a car, I enjoyed the walk.   At the half way point I could cut across the field and save about two hundred yards.   The field was about a hundred yards wide at that location and was the edge of a larger section of land that bordered the town on one side and, on the other, sloped down to the Mekong River.   The town had a small port on the river further to the south but here the river was a couple hundred yards away.   I had crossed the field on occasion during daylight as there were a few paths one could follow. At night, however, it was too dark to safely see what was on or near the path ahead of you, and night was when the snakes would be out.

On this night I had come to the point of decision and said what the hell, I'm not afraid and started across the field.   At first, the light from the town's edge along with the light from the partial moon made navigating feasible.   I had barely traveled a quarter of the way, however, when I stopped, realizing that I couldn't see anything on the path ahead of me. I could only tell I was still on the path as the grass and weeds were over a foot high on both sides of it.   My bravado had taken a big hit but I decided to keep going.   I had only taken four more steps when a rustle in the dry grass just next to me brought me to a quick halt.   I didn't know what had made the noise, but I decided to swallow my pride and turn around.

As I turned and started walking, another rustle and then a hissing sound reinforced my decision to retreat. I looked over my shoulder and saw what I thought to be two large cobra's with their heads about three off the ground watching me. My walk back to safety turned into a run.

In my dream the snakes were still there chasing me and it was harder and harder to keep running.

Suddenly I was partially back in the real world. My shoulder hurt, someone was moving me and talking to me. I knew it was Benny and I tried to ask him to leave me alone, to tell him he was hurting my shoulder, but I couldn't get the words out.

I returned slowly to my dream world. I was back in the snow chasing the apparition in white that I had chased the evening before. This time I caught up with her and as I grabbed hold of her she disappeared in a puff of smoke. All that was left was the red hat embroidered with a gold star lying at my feet. I leaned over to pick it up but my arm hurt too much to reach it.

The pain became less part of my dream and more a reality as I slowly awoke from my drug induced slumber. I was no longer on the bed but was now sitting on a wheelchair. I instinctively attempted to stand up but couldn't. Looking down I saw that my wrists and ankles had been secured to the wheel chair with duct tape. I tried to free them but couldn't. I had on the pants and shoes I had been wearing all day but now was also wearing a large red sweatshirt.

The Hamilton's had dressed me up for the party.

Chapter 21

I sat there staring at the door and trying to break free of the tape. It was useless. The duct tape stretched a little which gave me some hope, but ultimately not enough to make any progress towards getting my hands or legs free. Surprisingly my shoulder felt better in this position and the slight movement of my hands and arms didn't aggravate it.

At some point between my being shot and sitting there in the quiet I became confident that Melissa was there in that house with me. The idea seemed farfetched and insane, yet fit all the facts I knew about the case. I knew it had to be true, it just wasn't rational.

I also realized that if Melissa was there and alive, then I would be killed when she was. It was a fate I was determined not to accept for either of us but for the moment had no intelligent plan to avoid it.

The door started to open and my attention turned towards it. It opened only a few inches and stopped. I heard talking outside it. Mr. and Mrs. Hamilton were talking about the timing of the something, I surmised the party, as there was some questioning as to when the food would be ready.

The talking stopped and after a short pause the door opened the rest of the way. Bennie Hamilton stepped in smiling.

"How about homemade pizza for your last meal? Prissy

makes a knockout pepperoni and black olive pizza."

I wanted to knock the smirk off his face but kept my face neutral. "I like pizza, always have. I don't think Melissa does, though, shouldn't you be asking her?"

"You mean Jackie, don't you?" He said it with such a grin on his face that I knew he knew that I now knew what was going on.

"How did this ever start, Bennie? I knew you weren't very friendly but I never figured you to be nuts."

I sensed he wanted to strike out at me but resisted the urge. "So you think you have this figured out? Too bad that it took you this long. But you know sonny boy, if you're the best they have out there in the real world then you know why I'm not sweating."

"The sheriff's office knew I was coming out here today. You're just digging yourself into a deeper hole. They should be looking for me by now."

"I don't think so and even if they are I don't really care."

The way he said that made me wonder. Did he have a foolproof plan to get rid of us and avoid police scrutiny, or did he simply not care if he was caught?   It could be either one. I had nothing to lose, so decided to see if I could drag as much information out of him as possible. It couldn't hurt and as Sun Tzu preached – know thy enemy.

"What can you possibly get out of doing this? Let's accept that my comment earlier about your being nuts was made out of anger. What possibly can be your motivation for doing this? You must be in your late sixties," he actually looked a little older to me. "How did all this get started? Why would you start grabbing young women off the streets at this point of your life? I don't mean this to come across in the wrong way, but Benny, honestly, it was kind of late in life to decide to condemn yourself to an eternity in hell, wasn't it?"

"I don't believe in hell and I never grabbed a single woman off the streets. I did my best to prevent it, smart guy. You know, I don't even mind explaining all this to you. You don't have the little grey cells to figure it out on your own and it certainly won't change how your day will end."

I sat in silence waiting for him to continue. It didn't take long and once he started he seemed to want to talk about it.

"Our daughter fell off the cliff behind us seven years ago today. She was our only child. We didn't have her until later in life, after we had given up hope of having children. We looked at her birth as a miracle, and, yes, at that time we believed she was a gift from God. She was a good kid, a smart girl who brought us a lot of happiness and cheer. Prissy and Jackie had a special bond. You have to understand, she wasn't just her daughter, they were best friends. The two would talk for hours about what happened at school, about boys, whatever they wanted. Jackie had big plans for college. She wanted to become a doctor. Prissy had been a nurse and for Jackie to become a doctor would have been the ultimate success story. But then, seven years ago today, she fell to her death."

"I'm very sorry. I don't have any children but believe me I can understand the suffering you both must have gone through."

He looked at me like I didn't know anything but continued.

"Our lives changed that day. For Jackie to die like that on her birthday and just a few days before Christmas was like a sucker punch from God. We didn't celebrate Christmas that year nor have we ever since. It became obvious to me at that time that there was no God. If there was one he was cruel and didn't deserve my respect or concern. Hell is what he has already put us through, he couldn't do any worse. I'll welcome death when it comes."

There was no use my arguing and I wanted to get him to start talking about the girls and to move on from his self pity.

"I'm not that religious myself, and I can appreciate how you felt but I still don't understand how the girls ended up here."

"It was Prissy, not me. It never entered my mind. She took Jackie's death as hard as I did, maybe harder if that is possible. Our daughter was stolen from us. I suffered, but never did I think of grabbing some kid off the road and calling her Jackie. It was just shy of a year after Jackie's death, maybe a day or two before her birthday. I was here watching television and the door opens and in walks Prissy with a young lady. My first thought was how much the girl looked like Jackie. I thought it was just some young girl that Prissy knew from somewhere, who had come home with Prissy to help her do something.

"After saying hello, I continued watching television. Within a minute or two I could hear loud voices from the kitchen and something crashing onto the floor. I jumped up and went into the kitchen to see what was happening. There was Prissy hanging onto the girl's wrist shouting at her that she couldn't leave. She was calling her Jackie. It spooked me and I had to force Prissy into letting go. The girl went running out of the house. I ran after her and got her to stop at the street. I explained to her about our daughter's death and that Prissy must be having some sort of breakdown. She accepted my story and even allowed me to drive her back to town."

"Did she go to the police?"   I had not remembered anything similar in any of the investigative files I looked through.

"No, not that I ever heard of, she actually felt sorry for Prissy. I told her I would get Prissy some help but never did. Maybe I should have but that is all water under the bridge."

He said this last part almost with a sound of regret.

"Why did Prissy do it?"

"As I said, it was just a couple days before what would have been Jackie's birthday. To Prissy, that young girl was Jackie. In her mind Jackie had come home for her birthday."

"You mentioned that the girl was trying to get away from Prissy. Later after the girl was gone, did you talk to Prissy, how did she explain that?"

"She had no explanation for that or for anything since. On that occasion and ever since, to Prissy, each girl has been Jackie. When I got back home after taking the girl back to her hotel Prissy was in a great mood. She talked all night about how nice it was that Jackie had stopped by to say hello. I tried to get her to understand that what she had done was wrong and that Jackie was dead but I never could get through to her. The days went by and the only mention Prissy made relating to the event was a brief comment on Jackie's birthday that she wished Jackie could have stayed for her birthday. That was it. I thought the incident happened and was over."

"But it wasn't over, was it?" It was a rhetorical question but I wanted him to keep talking.

"No, it wasn't. For nearly a year, I thought it was. But then I returned home late one day from a shopping trip in

Roswell the following year, maybe three days before Jackie's birthday and found it had happened again. This time she had been a little more subtle. Like the previous year, she ran into a girl that looked a little bit like Jackie and had somehow decided it was Jackie. She used some ruse to get the girl to come to the house with her. This time, however, rather than just start calling her Jackie and freaking her out, she had drugged the girl and locked her in Jackie's room. That's not what Prissy said, of course, in her mind Jackie was just taking a nap."

"Why didn't you send this one back, just like the first?"

"That was my intent. I even told Prissy we had to let her go and despite Prissy begging me not to, I unlocked the bedroom door and went in to free the girl. Prissy went crying to our bedroom. There was a small table lamp on in the room but nothing else so the room was not very well lit. I walked over to the bed and had quite a shock. In that half light it did look like Jackie was there in that bed. The hair and facial features were just like my daughter's. Prissy had even dressed the girl in some of Jackie's pajamas."

"I imagine it was quite a shock for you. But what happened?" I asked.

"I began talking to her, trying to get her to come out of her stupor. She was very groggy. I tried sitting her up and I noticed right away she was a lot more developed than Jackie had been. Prissy had only been able to button the bottom two buttons of her pajama top. I tried to get the pajama top to better cover her up and to button at least one more button. She was regaining consciousness slowly and kept moving about."

I couldn't help but wonder how much of his assistance was above board and how much of it was actually fondling the semi-conscious young girl.

He continued. "All of a sudden she started screaming and flailing her arms. I tried to calm her down but she was strong. She was up and pushing and shouting at me. She kept saying she was going to report me to the police and tell them that I was trying to rape her. I was trying to hold onto her, I certainly didn't want her to leave in the state she was in. We tumbled around the room a few times before I fell and she broke free. She turned to the door and made about two steps before Prissy appeared out of nowhere and floored her with one punch."

"She hit her with her fist?"

"Yes. I don't believe Prissy ever struck Jackie other than maybe a few smacks on the hand or rear when she was young. It was right there and then, sitting on the floor next to that young girl lying there unconscious next to me that I realized the reality of my world had changed."

"I guess it had. How did Prissy feel about what had just occurred?"

He had reached the point now where he wanted to talk. I had seen it many times before. Many people who have done terribly wrong things conceal them from the world for a long time. They know speaking about them can bring instant damnation and subsequent punishment. When they finally open up it is normal for them to let all but the most damning come out. It's almost like tapping into a pressure relief valve for them to finally be able to talk about what they have been through and kept secret inside for so long.

"I remember exactly what Prissy said standing there over both of us. She said, 'Now I wonder what made her go to pieces like that?' I almost started laughing it was so unreal. Here we had kidnapped and terrified this young girl and

Prissy wondered what could have made her behave like that."

"But in your wife's defense," I responded, "she thought she was dealing with her daughter."

"That's right, you're exactly right Jim. She never wanted any of those girls to be harmed. In fact, in her mind Jackie is still alive and waiting in her room merrily for her party. Prissy has brought all this on us but will never understand or accept it. I've been down that road a number of times trying to convince her to stop bringing the girls home but she just can't help herself."

I wondered to myself how much of that was really true or just the dream world that Mrs. Hamilton knowingly put herself into when convenient. Punching your daughter out because she wants to leave home sounded a little out of character for the role she was allegedly not playing.

"I no longer thought it was possible to let her go." Benny started talking about the first victim again. "Her face was bleeding and was swelling fast, Prissy broke her nose. At least I thought she had. She was lying there stunned. I was afraid if we let her go, she would contact the police. She had already said she would."

"What did you do, Benny?"

"I didn't know what to do but Prissy did. She gave her something to keep her calm. It put her in a stupor. She was very groggy but not totally out of it. We had to feed her and help her with other things. I boarded up her window and we had to put a dead bolt on her door."

"How could that environment give Prissy any happiness at all? She has to understand what was going on."

"We talked about it, but I don't think Prissy ever really understood it. Each year she keeps talking about how she hopes Jackie will be feeling better by her birthday. To her they are always a little sick and she is just keeping them medicated."

"What happens at the birthday party?"

"You'll see," answered Benny. "It's really just your ordinary birthday dinner with a cake."

"But if the girls are drugged, it can't be much of a party."

"The girls are not given any medication the day of the party. They are still a bit groggy and disoriented but can function fairly well on their own."

"Why would they be cooperative in any way?" I asked.

"I have a long talk with them a few hours before the party. Even though they had been drugged, they know that Prissy kept referring to them as Jackie and they realize that Prissy has some, should we say, issues. They also know I have not done anything to hurt them."

Again, something in the way he said it made me wonder about how far he stretched the words 'hurt them.'

"I make it very clear to them that Prissy has a problem. I tell them about Jackie and that each year at this time it gets worse for Prissy. I tell them that we have stopped giving them the medication and that if they behave for the remainder of the day and especially during the party that I will let them go free after the party."

"Certainly they don't believe that you will just let them go free after what you put them through."

"I don't know how much any of them believed it. But what choice do they have? Better to try and see what happens than simply be kept a prisoner forever. Most were very cooperative and, as you'll soon see for yourself, even though they weren't given any medication on Jackie's birthday, they each were still affected a little by it. They weren't zombies like they had been but they are still a little shaky. You'll see. You say you know this one?"

"Just barely, I know her parents." I didn't want to give him anything to use against me.

Despite my denial, he still tried. "Well then, Jim, you best behave at the party too. You behave and you'll go quick and painless with a bullet through the back of your head. It will look like a Mafia hit, or so the television shows imply. More importantly, the girl's death will be quick. You misbehave and she will suffer and you'll get to watch. You wouldn't want that, would you?"

"You make it sound like you're doing me a favor. I hope I can make it as easy as possible for you."

He stared at me and then looked down at his watch. Mine was gone and I had no idea what time it was.

"What time is it and what time is the party?" I asked.

"We've got about an hour. Don't worry you won't be late."

"How do I go to the bathroom all tied up like this?"

"You don't," was all he said.

Lucky for me, I thought, I hadn't eaten much that day and had very little to drink.

"It must be hard for you to get the girls out to the ledge. They must know something isn't right long before they get all the way out there."

"Actually that's the easy part. It's also the part you don't need to worry yourself with. Although I have to admit your being here does complicate matters quite a bit. Double the workload, I guess you could say."

"I think you are actually enjoying this, aren't you Benny? All this blame on Prissy makes it easy for you to rationalize what you are doing. I think you are pretty sick yourself.

How many of the girls did you not hurt by raping them? You know Benny, I'm beginning to think you are just a dirty old pervert. I bet you encouraged Prissy to bring those girls home for you."

I could see the anger mount within Benny. He suddenly stepped forward and slapped me hard across my face. I winced, not because of the impact with my face, but because of the pain the sudden movement of my head and neck had on my shoulder.

He must have enjoyed what he saw because he struck me three or four more times, tiring himself out. He stepped back, glared at me and walked out.

I wasn't sure what caused me to anger Benny. I wanted to know what pushed his buttons but I also wanted to keep him talking. By getting him mad, I cancelled any chances at the second goal and was not sure if I learned much more about him. If I had to make a bet, I would bet that he never raped any of the girls. There was nothing in the police reports relating to any sexual activity, forced or otherwise prior to death. Considering the length of time between death and discovery, though, such a diagnosis might not have been possible.

I stopped thinking about Benny and started thinking about Melissa and how I was going to get us out of this mess. I didn't have a solution and needed one soon. Talking my way out wasn't a possibility. I would just have to be ready to improvise when opportunity presented itself and that meant staying alert for when it did.

I could hear Benny and Prissy talking and the normal kitchen noises one would make moving dishes and utensils around. It sounded like they might be emptying a dishwasher, although I had not heard one running earlier. I listened for Melissa but didn't hear anything that would give me any indication where she was in the house or how she was. She couldn't be far away, the house wasn't that big.

Benny had said that they wouldn't be giving Melissa any more drugs today so depending how powerful or long lasting the stuff was she should slowly become more alert. They wanted her to be able to function on her own at the birthday party, but I thought they probably also had an ulterior motive. The longer she was off the stuff, the less likely it would be picked up in an autopsy.

I wondered what they might be using to drug Melissa but decided it didn't really matter. There was nothing I could do about it. I had to deal with her condition as it was. Hopefully she would be alert enough to help, or at least not hinder me when the time came for action.

The odd ball in the mix was Mrs. Hamilton. How much did she really believe that the girls were Jackie? Was she totally oblivious to the fact that these girls weren't really her daughter or was there a little nugget of knowledge suppressed somewhere just below the surface? She had to be somewhat crazy just to do what she did, but how crazy? That was the question, and the follow on was whether I could use it to my advantage.

On the other hand, she knew her husband shot me and seemed to accept that fact without any concern. Bringing me in and patching me up so I could attend her dead daughter's birthday party did lend support to the argument she was nuts.

As I sat there trying to formulate a strategy, any strategy that might help us to escape, I began to hear the muffled sound of people talking. I couldn't interpret what was being said but one of the voices sounded like that of a young women. It only lasted a minute or so.

I strained to hear more but everything was quiet. The voices had come from the far side of the house. I tried to picture the house in my mind. I knew what it looked like from the outside but only had partial knowledge of the interior. There was a small hallway from the front door that ended in what I believed was the living or family room. As you enter the house, the first room on the left was the sitting room or den where Benny had met with Peter and me on our first visit. Across the hall and a little closer to the front door was the closet with the red and yellow hat. Although I never saw it, I had the impression from my first visit that the kitchen was just before the living room to the left of the hall.

From the sounds of dishes I had heard earlier this would put me to the right of the hall opposite the kitchen. My window was probably on the front of the house facing the street. I had seen one there and it made sense that it was a bedroom window. The room Melissa was in was on the other side of the house possibly located behind the garage.

The voices were there again this time louder. Two women's voices, one of them higher pitched. I could sense anger or fear in the voice I attributed to Melissa. The voices suddenly stopped. Then I thought I could hear the older woman, Prissy I was sure, talking softly again. After a few seconds everything was quiet.

I almost shouted out Melissa's name. I had a strong urge to communicate with her, to tell her to hang in there, but I knew that it would be counterproductive. Instead I refocused my mind towards escape. If I could break free of the duct tape I would at least have a chance. Even though Benny had a weapon and his mind seemed sharp, he was much older than me and I was sure I could easily over power him. In fact, Prissy appeared to be the stronger of the two. I could easily envision her punching out the first victim just as Benny had described.

Prissy would present a different dilemma. I was aware of dozens of examples where a woman had stolen a small baby from a hospital, a mall, and even from someone's home in order to make the child their own. But I couldn't think of a single incident where the victim was eighteen to twenty years old.

On the one hand, Prissy might just wave good bye and give us some cake to take with us as we walked out the door. On the other, she might totally freak out. But I would never know unless I could somehow get free of the tape that kept me bound to the wheelchair.

Looking around the room, I saw nothing that could be used to cut the tape. I tried moving the chair to get a look at the rest of the room but was unable to reach either wheel with my fingers. I sat there impotent and frustrated.

The storm outside sounded as though it was getting worse. I could hear the wind now and hadn't noticed it earlier. The house shuddered when some of the gusts of wind struck it. And while I didn't know it at the time, the snow had gotten even heavier. Although the house was warm, I involuntarily shivered.

It seemed like I sat there forever before Benny came back in the room.

"Are you ready?" He asked with that stupid grin on his face again.

"Is my hair combed?" I asked sarcastically.

"Good enough," was his response as he walked behind the wheelchair and began pushing me out of the room.

My mental configuration of the house turned out to be

fairly accurate. Benny pushed me out of the room into a small hallway and we turned to the left. The end of this hallway brought us into a moderately sized great room, the portion we entered served as a living room and the far end as a dining room. On the far wall, straight ahead of me there was another hallway that I imagined led to the room where Melissa was being kept. Benny steered me towards the dining room table. We passed the hallway to my left that led to the front door and I caught a quick glance of the kitchen through its entrance from the front hallway. As we got closer to the table I saw the kitchen also had a doorway that gave it access directly to the dining room.

The dining room area was decorated with a few balloons and a banner across the wall opposite the kitchen that said Happy Birthday. The table was big enough for six but only four place settings had been arranged at the end of table furthest from the kitchen. Benny pushed me up to the one place setting on this side of the table and then walked to the kitchen directly to my left. I realized that the white table cloth was actually made of paper.

I looked around. The blinds were drawn and the lights had been turned on. No one else was in the room. There were two place settings across the table and one to my right at the end of the table. I assumed Benny would be to my right and Melissa and Prissy would be across from me. I looked at the banner to my right. It looked old and I couldn't help but wonder if it dated back to Jackie's lifetime.

We would be using plastic knives and forks and eating off paper plates that said Happy Birthday in pink. I heard a toilet flush behind me, but otherwise everything was quiet. I had found myself in many strange situations in the past but this had to be the most bizarre.

"They should be out momentarily," Benny said from somewhere behind me.

I didn't bother trying to turn around.

"I hope so, I'm getting a little hungry." I wasn't really. I just wanted everything to stay in "role" for as long as possible.   I knew once the party was over, crunch time would start.

Chapter 22

In a few minutes I could hear voices down the hall from where I believed Melissa was being kept. People were moving as the voices seemed to be getting closer. Suddenly she was there entering the dining room. I had no doubt that the young lady was Melissa. Even though I had not seen her since she was a child, I knew it was her. I could see aspects of both John and Martha in her.

Melissa looked at me without any recognition or, for that matter, any emotion at all. She was unsteady in her walk and Prissy was following close behind her supporting Melissa by grabbing one of her arms every few steps. She guided her to the side of the table opposite me.

I instinctively felt the urge to stand up and help her but could only sit there. The scene was eerie, almost frightening. Prissy had on a flowered dress that appeared to be a copy, other than the size, of the one Melissa was wearing. Mother and daughter had dressed alike. Additionally, both had on bright red lipstick that did not seem to match anything but each other.

"Your chair is the one further down Jackie," Prissy instructed as Melissa tried to sit in the first chair. "You get to sit across from your friend Jim. Wasn't it nice for him to come to your party?"

Melissa did not respond, but did look at me suddenly with what looked like curiosity. I noticed something I didn't see at first when she entered the room. Her left eye was swollen slightly and despite the makeup I thought I could see some bruising around it. The left half of her upper lip also looked like it was a little puffy. I guessed that she had not been the perfectly obedient daughter. Despite feeling some sympathy for her, it also gave me some hope she could be a fighter if necessary.

She didn't sit down right away but glanced over at the Happy Birthday banner tacked to the wall. She then looked down at the paper plates.

I figured Melissa was a little over five and a half feet tall with a medium build. Her hair was blond and more than shoulder length. She was wearing it straight down. She had blue eyes that still looked like she was still under some of the effects of the medication.

I glanced back at Prissy who was still holding on to Melissa's right arm and noticed that even their eye shadow matched. I didn't know if the likeness was because Prissy only had one type of lipstick and eye shadow or if she just wanted mother and daughter to look alike. A goal totally unreachable as I guessed Prissy had her by at least one hundred and fifty pounds.

"Jim, cat got your tongue? Say hello to Jackie."

I tried to put on my most sincere face. "Hello Jackie, I'm Jim West. I met you a long time ago. We went fishing once, do you remember?"

I noticed a subtle shaking of her head. I took it for a no. I didn't imagine she would have remembered it even in better circumstances.

"Well, aren't you going to wish her Happy Birthday?" Prissy asked me in a way I took more as an order.

"Sure I was, Happy Birthday Jackie."

Still no response.

"Sit down Jackie. Your Dad will be bringing out the hot dogs any time now. I never could understand why you always just want hot dogs and beans on your birthday. Maybe next year we'll do something different like pizza. Your Dad always wants me to make pizza. I just tell him this is your party not his." She looked at me after Melissa sat down. "Jim, I sure hope you don't mind hot dogs."

"No, I like them just fine."

Prissy moved around behind Melissa and pushed her chair in and then, in a fairly quick motion, looped what looked like a bath robe belt around Melissa. She pulled it snug, with the belt tightening just under Melissa's breasts, and tied it behind the chair.

"That will help you stay upright in the chair, sugar. You've been sick the last few days and we don't want you fainting and falling out of the chair. Just let me know if it gets uncomfortable." After securing the belt, Prissy wondered off towards the kitchen muttering, "Where's that food?"

The belt would be fairly easy for most people to free themselves but Melissa made no effort. She followed Prissy out of the room with her eyes and then looked at me. She didn't say anything.

I glanced at the kitchen door and saw no one. I could hear Benny and Prissy talking. I looked back at Melissa and whispered, "Melissa, I am your friend, are you okay?"

Again there was no answer except a barely perceptible nod which I took for a yes. I was going to say something more but was interrupted by Benny and Prissy coming out of the kitchen with our dinner.

He carried a bowl of steaming pork and beans and she carried a plate of hot dogs and a plate of buns. The ketchup and mustard were already on the table.

They both took their seats. I wasn't too sure how I was supposed to eat and seriously doubted they would be freeing one or both of my hands.

"Here Jackie, take yourself a hot dog and bun," Prissy said as she held out the plate of hot dogs. The buns were already in front of Melissa.

Melissa reached up slowly and with a slight tremor in her hands took a bun and placed a hot dog into it. She put it on her plate without taking a bite.

"Let me give you some beans, they're your favorite." Prissy put a large spoonful of beans onto Melissa's plate. The sauce in the beans quickly spread over the plate and started soaking into one end of the hot dog bun.

Melissa sat there unemotionally and watched everything evolve. She made no effort to start eating.

"How about you Jim, one or two hot dogs?"

"Just one. Thank you, Mrs. Hamilton."

"Ketchup or mustard on your dog?"

"Just mustard, please." So Prissy at least understood that I couldn't serve myself. Again I wondered where her insanity and reality fit together.

She put a large amount of mustard on the bun, plopped on a hot dog and sat it on my plate.

Both Hamilton's then served themselves and started eating.

"Jackie, are you dating anyone? You know you broke a lot of hearts in high school. It's certainly time for you to start taking boys seriously." Prissy talked with food in her mouth so some of her words came out slurred. "Not that we are in a hurry for grandchildren, Jackie, but your Dad and I aren't getting any younger. It would be nice. You know your

Aunt Kathleen has six grandchildren."

"Don't be silly, Prissy, your sister had five children, too, and all of them are older than Jackie." After saying this, Benny looked at me and rolled his eyes as if to say 'Can you believe she is saying this?'

They're both nuts, I thought. Melissa simply continued staring at her plate of food.

"Hurry up and eat your hot dog before it becomes a cold dog Jackie." Prissy gave a little laugh at her joke. "Come on, now, you need your strength to get better." Prissy nudged Melissa's arm and Melissa responded by picking up the hot dog and taking a bite of the end that the bean sauce hadn't spoiled. She chewed slowly and looked at me. I thought I could see a tear developing in her left eye. Maybe it was just my imagination as no tear fell from either eye.

"You'd better eat now like your Momma says," instructed Benny sounding a little more ominous than Prissy had. As he said it, he put his hand under the table and touched Melissa in some way or some place that made her physically cringe for a second. "Remember our conversation," he said softly.

I wanted to pound my fist into Benny's wrinkled face, but all I could do was talk and thereby hope to get some of the attention off Melissa.

"Jackie, I'm sorry that I was unable to bring your birthday present with me today, but I'll get it to you as soon as I can."

"Oh, that's nice of you Jim," remarked Prissy. "Your father and I think you are too old for presents now. Don't you think so, Jackie? The world has become so commercialized. I think this party and just being together as a family is the best thing for all. I know it means so much to me."

My eye focused on the plastic knife next to my plate moments before my conscious mind caught up with it. I didn't know if the serrated edge of the knife could cut the duct tape but if I could just get it in my hand I sure wanted to give it a try. I reached out with my fingers and tried to grab the table cloth. I could touch it but not get a good enough grip to pull it towards me. The knife was perfectly lined up with my right hand but I couldn't get to it. If I could pull the table cloth towards me about four inches the knife would just drop into my hand.

I knew that even if I could get a grip on the table cloth, Benny would certainly notice my pulling it towards me that far. It felt like a sucker's bet, but I couldn't think of anything else and with the knife sitting right there I had to try.

I wiggled and rocked my body in the chair so much that Benny asked me what was the matter.

"I'm just cramping up a little, it will pass. I know you don't want to feed me, but if you push me in a little I might be able to lean over and just eat without my hands."

Benny leaned towards me. "Maybe I'll feed you some cake later," he said in a whisper that failed to exude any hint of sympathy.

"What's that Benny?" Prissy asked.

"Oh, nothing dear. Jim just said he didn't feel much like eating, maybe he'll just have some cake later."

"Well," I started to say when I was roughly kicked on my right shin. I looked over at Benny who was staring at me. I took the hint and shut up. My shin hurt. Benny must be wearing boots.

I looked up at Melissa. She was watching me. How much of her mind was still fighting the cobwebs from the drugs and how much had become lucid? I sensed she was at least starting to get a grasp on what was going on. She must know by now that I am a prisoner like her and therefore on her side.

Melissa had eaten half her hot dog and had started on her beans. Good for you, I thought. The food should help you. Melissa was eating slowly but she was eating. She had not said a word though throughout the entire meal. If I was her parent, that would have bothered me but both Hamilton's seemed to be fine with her silence.

Prissy and Benny finished before Melissa. My plate still hadn't been touched, so I guess that made me last.

Prissy told a story about a birthday party years ago when Jackie was twelve and several of her friends were in attendance. Everyone had so much cake and ice cream that one of the boys had thrown up all over the dining room rug before the party was over. Both Prissy and Benny laughed out loud talking about it. I didn't but I guessed you had to be there to see the humor.

Finally, Prissy noticed that Melissa had stopped eating. "Guess it's time for the cake," she said and stood up. "I'll be right back."

Prissy first gathered up the plates, thankfully leaving the knives and forks behind on the table, and then proceeded to the kitchen. In just a few seconds, she returned with a sheet cake with white frosting and a bunch of candles sticking up out of it.

"Benny, can I get your help in lighting the candles?"

"Sure, dear," Benny stood up and went behind me. He appeared next to her at the end of the table with an extended lighter. He was quick with the lighter and it seemed like only a minute before all the candles were lit.

Prissy put the cake in front of Melissa and announced that the three of us would sing Happy Birthday and

Melissa's job was to blow out the candles when we finished singing. She then reached over and turned off the overhead light. The lamps in the living room still gave us some relief but the candles glowed brightly in the shadows.

Prissy started the song and Benny joined in immediately. They both stared at me and despite the surreal environment I felt the best thing I could do was to join in. There I was, duct taped to a wheelchair with two crazies singing happy birthday to a person who was supposed to be their daughter but who, at least one of them knew, was really seven years dead tonight. My only solace was to try to imagine what was Melissa thinking at this point?

As the song ended, to my surprise, Melissa leaned over and tried to blow out the candles. She even seemed to have a slight smile on her face. That made me worry, but hopefully she was just role playing.

She only got about half of them out, but Prissy clapped her hands in glee and leaned over blowing the rest out. She gave Melissa a quick hug and announced, "Time to cut the cake."

I noticed that Melissa hadn't returned the hug. Other than the fact that she had just blown out some of the candles, Melissa had been a non-entity during the entire party. I was a little surprised that neither Benny nor Prissy seemed to mind. Go to all that effort to kidnap a girl and then pretend she's your daughter and she just sits there during the big birthday event. Perhaps they had tried to get the first one or two to be involved and it had backfired. Maybe it was better to have the make believe Jackie sit there quietly than to yell and scream to be let free. After all wasn't passivity over negativity what tyrants appreciated the most from their subjects.

Prissy had produced a large nasty looking knife from somewhere and started cutting slices of birthday cake. She must have carried the knife out with her when she brought out the cake but I didn't see it. The blade must have been a foot long. It could have been a large bread knife except it had a sharp point.

"You like knives, Jim?" Benny must have seen me staring.

"Not particularly, Benny."

"Well do let me know if you prefer them over guns." Again he had that little smirk on his face that I would love to have the opportunity to knock off.

"Depends on the situation, I guess," was my answer.

"Would you like a big piece of cake or a little piece, Jackie?" Prissy asked.

"Just a little piece, please," answered Melissa to my surprise. I looked at Prissy but saw no reaction. That was reasonable, I realized, in the days she had been here they would have had a number of conversations with her. It was just me, hearing her voice for the first time, who was affected.

Melissa's voice sounded almost normal. I don't know if I expected hysteria, anger, a slurring distortion caused by the drugs or what, but her voice sounded okay with maybe just a hint of fatigue.

Prissy first gave Melissa her piece and then put mine in front of me. White cake with white frosting, I actually wouldn't have minded eating it. Melissa picked up her fork and began eating her cake right away. She kept her eyes down just looking at the cake while she was eating.

"Prissy," Benny asked, "did you hear anything on the radio today about the weather? Last I heard it was supposed to go on snowing like this through tomorrow night. Maybe get a foot of snow in all."

"They said something about it this morning. I wasn't paying too much attention but that is what I thought I heard too. I know it's blowing and snowing hard out there right now." She then turned her head towards me. "I never have liked it here in the blizzards. Isn't that silly of me? I have lived here nearly my whole life and have never liked the blizzards. You think I would have moved to Florida years ago."

"I told you a number of times I'd take you there, Prissy, but you never wanted to move." Benny sounded as though he was tired of hearing her say this.

"I know. That's what I'm saying. I don't like the winter storms but won't do anything about it. That's just silly, don't you think?"

"Stubborn, more like it," Benny responded with a laugh.

"More cake, Jackie?" Prissy asked.

Melissa just shook her head no.

"You know, Benny, with the weather like it is maybe you should let Jackie spend another night here with us."

"I don't think that would really work out. Jackie and I have already talked about it and she really would like to get home. Isn't that right Jackie?"

"Yes, I would."   There was a little more tension in Melissa's voice.

"Oh, I just hate only seeing you a couple days a year. I think you should move back in with us, at least until you get married."

"Now dear," Benny talked softly to his wife, "you know Jackie has a job and a life of her own now. She needs to get going pretty soon."

"Prissy," I jumped into this conversation, "your husband's right, and I'll need to go with them when they do.

You know, ma'am, you have such a nice house and this has been such a nice party, I hate to go, too. In fact, Prissy, if you would just undo the tape on my wrists I can drive Jackie back to her house. That way Benny doesn't even have to travel in this terrible weather."

I noticed Melissa watching me while I was talking.

"Now Jim, I don't mind going out in this kind of weather. I told you that earlier. Besides, I don't know you well enough to let my daughter get in a car with you and drive off on a night like this. That would simply be irresponsible of me."

"Mom," it was Melissa. Everyone stopped talking and looked at her. "There is no reason for dad to drive on a night like tonight. I'll be okay going with Jim."

I think everyone was so surprised by Melissa's joining in that nobody said anything for a moment. Her comments made me aware that she was back from any kind of stupor the drugs may have had her in. She had figured out that I was a prisoner like her and she had called Prissy 'Mom'. That had to have an impact on Prissy.

Prissy reached out with her left hand and rested it gently on Melissa's right arm. "How about that, Benny?"

Benny stayed calm. "Dear, it's nice of both Jackie and Jim to want to save me the trouble, but if Jim would just think for a second, he came here this morning because his car battery had died." He had me there, I had forgotten.

"Oh that's right," Prissy said in agreement. "Wasn't it good luck that your battery lasted long enough to get you here to the party before it died?"

"So that's that." Benny stated and stood up. "Prissy can you take Jackie and help her change back into her traveling clothes. You know the outfit she was wearing when she came here. I'll stay here and keep Jim company until you come back."

Prissy untied the belt behind Melissa's back and stood up still holding on to Melissa's arm. Melissa had little choice but to stand up too. They both walked out of the room.

I could only imagine what was going through Melissa's mind. No doubt she was terrified but she was probably clinging to some hope too. She may not have suffered any serious harm, just kept prisoner by a couple of crazy old people. She had been told that she would be allowed to go home and now they were telling her to get back into her own outfit to be taken home. No doubt she wanted to believe she would be set free, but there had to be a tidal wave of suspicion that they were lying to her.

I wondered if she could take Benny in a fair fight. She probably could but I doubted if he would give her the chance. Still he had to get her to the ridge and that would give her a shot at getting away. Had they misdiagnosed and taken her off the medication too early? I thought so and certainly hoped they had.

"You're not listening to me." I realized Benny was talking to me. "Right after I have disposed of my daughter, I will come back for you. You know, I never have enjoyed doing away with the girls. I actually regret it. But you, my man, I am going to enjoy. You know, I said I was going to shoot you, but now I'm not so sure. I think I'll take the knife along with us when we go. Maybe I can be a little more imaginative. What do you think?"

"I think you're nuts."

He laughed out loud. "I'm sure I am."

He stood up and walked out to the kitchen. I struggled with the duct tape and tried again to grab the table cloth. I couldn't reach it. The knife sat there in the same spot, almost mocking me.

Benny came back out of the kitchen and yelled down the hall, "Hurry up you two."

He then sat down at the far end of the table. For someone who was about to kill two people Benny looked pretty calm.

"It's not too late to let us go, Benny." I knew it was a useless thing to say but there really wasn't much I could do but talk at the moment.

"You're just wasting your breath, Jim. If you keep talking I'll just have to use some more of that tape and tape your mouth shut."

I decided to be quiet. I didn't care if he put tape on my mouth or not, but I didn't want to be moved away from the table and the plastic knife. We sat there in silence for about five more minutes.

He must have seen Melissa and Prissy coming as he stood up and turned facing the hall. Melissa walked out first wearing jeans and a heavy, sky blue ski jacket. She was carrying a stocking cap that matched the jacket. I didn't see any gloves but if she had any they could have been in her pockets.

Benny took her by one hand, "I bet you are ready to be leaving here, aren't you?" He said it softly but I heard him. "You know when I was your age I couldn't stand to be at my parents' house for more than a few days at a time."

Melissa nodded and I thought I even saw a hint of a smile on her face. I hoped she hadn't convinced herself all was going to be okay.

Benny led her by the hand into the kitchen. I tried to force my right arm forward through the duct tape making some progress but at the expense of a couple layers of skin.

All three were in the kitchen and I tried rocking, bouncing and stretching in the chair with minimal success. With my fingers stretched out I could touch the table cloth but I couldn't grip it.

I heard Bennie and Prissy talking in the kitchen, something about the weather I thought. I did not hear Melissa but didn't expect to.

As no one was in the room, I tried a different approach. I leaned over my plate and with my head tried to reach the knife. It was awkward and aggravated my ribs and the bullet wound, but I was able to get my face down to the knife. Moving the knife to the edge of the table with any part of my face that would work caused me to contort myself to the extreme. The knife finally fell off the table and into my waiting right hand. I was just sitting myself back upright when I heard Mrs. Hamilton.

"Jim, what in the world, are you doing?"

"Prissy," I answered thinking fast, "you know for some reason Benny taped my hands to the wheel chair. I never had a chance to taste the cake so I thought, since I was alone, I might just lean over and have a bite. I tried but my shoulder hurt too much to let me reach the cake. Would you mind taking off this tape, or at least put a little on my fork and help me eat it?"

I could see the suspicion in her eyes. She walked over and pulled me away from the table. She briefly looked at the tape and then picked up the cake and fork and walked off to the kitchen.

"I'm not sure why Benny wanted you strapped in, but we'd best let him make the decision when to take the tape off." The last of these words were said as she entered the kitchen and again went out of sight.

I had palmed the knife as she was checking me over and now was carefully configuring the knife in my hand and under the tape so I could try and cut the tape. Using a sawing motion progress seemed to be very slow in coming. Finally, I could see the end of the tape start to split.

Just then though Prissy came back into the room. By necessity I had been cutting the lower inside of the tape on my right hand. I didn't think she could see anything, but stopped cutting as a precaution while she was in the room.

"Jim, you said your wound was bothering you, maybe I should get some medicine for you to help you relax. It would just be the same stuff I gave you earlier. Helps you sleep, too." She walked back behind me.

I turned my head to follow her as far as I could. "Prissy, you may want to hold off on that until after Benny gets back. I think he wanted to discuss some things with me when he returned. I need to stay alert."

"We'll see, I'll just get my things in case he thinks it would be a good idea."

My peripheral vision lost sight of her and I started cutting frantically at the tape. The last thing I needed was another dosage of her knock out juice. I almost cried when the plastic knife finally sliced its way through the tape. I considered putting the knife down and trying to peel off the tape on my left wrist but decided to stick with the little knife. This tape gave away quicker as I had a better angle with the knife. I leaned down and attacked the tape around my ankles with the knife, all the time glancing backwards.

The tape was finally off and I stood up stiff and sore. I had to hold onto the table for a second for balance but I knew I had no time to spare. I went towards the kitchen and caught the sight of Prissy coming out of the hallway to my left carrying a syringe.

"Jim, what are you doing?" She asked more surprised than angry.

"Don't worry. I'll be back, thanks." I replied and kept moving.

Back with the police, I thought. First though I had to find Melissa. There was a third doorway out of the kitchen that went into a laundry room that appeared to also serve as a mud room. It had a door to the outside and additional interior space where people could come in and get out of their boots and wet clothing without tramping through the house with them. This had to be the way they left.

I shot out the door. My first thought was of the cold and the darkness. I didn't have a coat on and could have also used a flashlight. But there was no turning back. There wasn't time and I didn't want to run back into Mrs. Hamilton.

Closing the door, I took a quick look around. There was a an exterior light by the door and despite its being covered with snow, it gave off enough light that I could see where the fresh snow had been disturbed just a few feet from the doorway. From there I could see a distinct set of sled tracks heading off towards the ridge. Inside the two tracks it looked like something else being dragged also was leaving a wider but less distinct track.

I took a step off the porch and noticed something else, a patch of red adjacent to the spot where the snow was disturbed. Blood, it was blood. Had he already killed her? Instinctively, I felt being watched and spun around. Just a couple feet from my face, I saw Prissy looking out through the glass at me. Her eyes sent chills down my spine and I took off running.

Chapter 23

I ran only partially to get away from her. Mostly I ran to catch up with Melissa and Benny. It was dark, but the tracks and Benny's foot prints were visible at my feet. When I looked up I couldn't see anything, but looking down I could follow the tracks. They went straight which helped me move faster. Benny knew where he was going.

At the edge of the ridge the tracks veered to the right, upwards and towards the Acorn's property. In my haste I couldn't stop where the tracks turned and found myself half sliding off the edge. I had to drop to my knees and grab at the ground with both hands in my effort not to go off over the ledge. By the time I came to a halt there wasn't more than six inches of dirt and snow between me and nothingness as I strained to see anything, down or up, in that direction. I literally crawled back to the sled tracks and started a more cautious trot.

My hands were wet and the cold really started to set in. I put both hands in my pants pockets in an effort to keep them thawed. My ears started to hurt. The cross wind was vicious and the snow was nearly blinding. I concentrated on looking down and moving. I needed to move fast enough to catch up as quickly as possible but not so fast that I go flying off the ridge as I had almost already done.

How far up was he taking her? Too far and I'd probably freeze to death, not far enough and he would have tossed her over the ridge before I could catch him. I tried to stop thinking and kept focused on moving. There was no other option.

I don't know how long it was that I kept going but all of a sudden I was literally on top of them both. I sensed their presence before I actually saw them and, as before at the ridge, could not stop before crashing into them.

He was bent over in an effort to pick Melissa's prone body up off the sled. He never saw me coming. Realizing I wasn't going to be able to stop without slipping and losing control I just let myself slam into him.   I wasn't moving that fast but he was off balance and the result we both went sprawling into the snow. Fortunately for me, the shock of pain from the bullet wound and already sore ribs brought my mind out of the numbing cold and quickly back into focus. I jumped to my feet aware that somewhere very close to me was the drop off to certain death but I was so disoriented I didn't know in which direction.   I looked around and saw Benny struggling in the snow to stand up.

I closed in on him and smashed my right fist into the side of his head. It wasn't as solid a blow as I would have liked as I didn't have good footing and we were both moving, but it knocked him back a few steps. He looked at me, snow from his fall caked against the left side of his face.

"You're too late," he said with that stupid smirk on his face again, "she's already dead."

As soon as I glanced to my left, I realized he was just trying to stall my attack.   Looking back at him, I saw him fighting with his heavy jacket to get to the revolver he had holstered around his waist. I dove at him as he drew the gun. In the snow it felt like I was moving in slow motion. The roar of a round going off was deafening and the flash was like lightning in my face.

I wasn't sure if the bullet hit me or not but either way, it didn't slow me down. I collided with him and we both went sprawling and then rolling on the snow covered ground. He was trying everything he could to get away from me and I just wanted to kill him.

Benny kicked and squirmed almost out of my grasp as we half crawled and half rolled around on the ground. I didn't know where the gun was but knew it wasn't in his hands. I also didn't know if he knew where it was and was trying to get to it. I was stronger than he was but my left arm was next to useless and my hands were numb. As he slithered and rolled to get away from me, I squirmed and crawled on my knees to catch up with him. I leapt at him with my right hand stretched out to grab at his throat, catching it as he disappeared with a scream from my view.

For a brief moment I didn't want to let go and Benny's falling body pulled me to the edge of the cliff. I let go of Benny's throat and tried to stabilize myself. Suddenly, whatever snow and earth my right leg was being supported by broke off and my right leg, like my right arm was dangling in the darkness. I thought I felt something give under my stomach and immediately rolled to my left. A lightning bolt of pain shot through me again as I did so and I knew I had finally torn open the stitching that had kept the bullet wound closed.

I laid there momentarily dazed looking up at the darkness and blowing snow. Forcing myself to stand up, I looked around for Melissa and the sled. I couldn't see it in the darkness but I knew it couldn't be far away. I moved away from the edge towards the center of the trail. The snow was disturbed all around me from our struggle but I knew I had to move downhill a few yards to get to the sled.

Putting my numb hands in my pockets seemed like a futile effort to keep them warm but I did so anyway. I knew Melissa and I had to get to somewhere warm fast or the cold would finish the job Benny had started.

Taking about ten steps, I reached the spot where I had run into Benny and Melissa and where the sled was supposed to be. Somehow, though, in that collision the sled had been spun around and had started going downhill by itself. Crouching down I could see the extra set of tracks in the snow. At first, as I followed them, they moved diagonally away from the edge of the cliff. That was good. But as I followed them further they started to veer back onto the main part of the trail and diagonally back towards the ridgeline.

I picked up my pace. Once again I was chasing these damn sled tracks not knowing what I would find. The wind was still howling and visibility had not gotten any better. It was hard to tell how hard the snow was falling or how much was being blown around by the wind. The original tracks were already being covered by the blowing snow. I knew I had to find Melissa quickly if we had any hope of finding our way back by way of the original tracks. In these conditions there was no other way I would be able to find shelter.

I realized the tracks were approaching the edge only when I noticed the snow on the ground disappearing a few feet to my right. I slowed down to have more control over my own momentum. The tracks continued right up to the edge where it appeared that the sled hit a three foot boulder and veered back to the left. I was relieved until I saw the sled now stationary a few yards away.

Melissa wasn't on it. Had the collision with the rock been sufficient to knock her off and over the edge? Was she even on the sled as it started its downhill slide? I should have looked around before I started after it. I looked back towards the edge and then back up the hill. I knew there was no way I could go back and look for her. I was already too cold and the tracks leading us back to the house would soon be hidden below the snow.

"No!" I yelled out in vain at the elements. How could I have come this close only to lose her? I knew my only chance was to get back to the house and call for help. I dreaded going back there and facing Prissy. She was insane, I had no doubt, but I didn't know how dangerous she actually was. She hadn't killed anyone yet, as far as I knew.

I turned and tried to focus on finding the original tracks. They were right in front of me, a bit of luck, I thought. I started a slow jog and took about five steps before my foot hit something and I tripped sprawling face first. Cold snow went shooting down the front of my sweatshirt and covered my face.

I sat up brushing the snow out of my face and saw a foot sticking awkwardly up in the air in my direction. I had tripped over a leg. Scrambling rapidly over to it I found the rest of the body. It was Melissa. I couldn't tell immediately if she was still alive but I knew she had moved to this spot from the sled and so she had to have been alive just moments before.

Kneeling next to her, I raised her to a sitting position.

"Melissa, wake up, Melissa."

I noticed her hat was gone and her hair was matted and sticky, not from the snow. Even in the darkness I could tell she suffered a severe blow to the back of her head. That was how he got them to the ridgeline without a struggle. He would hit them with something, probably just a large rock to knock them unconscious. He would them drop them over the side where they would hit more rocks disguising the truth behind the first wound.

"Melissa!" I shouted this time. "It's me, Jim. I'm here to help you."

I needed her up and moving as I did not think I could carry her all the way back.

She mumbled something. I had no idea what she tried to say but it was still music to my ears. She was alive.

"Everything is going to be okay now. Your real parents, John and Martha, sent me here to find you. I am your friend. Hang in there and we'll get to a hospital."

She mumbled something like "Mom," and passed back out.

I tried to pick her up but couldn't. Between the cold, my wounds and fatigue, I was about done myself. I knew the bullet wound had started bleeding again but didn't know how much blood I had lost.

Suddenly the obvious somehow penetrated my thick skull. The sled, I could use the sled to pull Melissa back to the house. That would be a lot easier and faster than carrying her.

"I'll be back in one second." I doubted if she heard me but I couldn't just walk away from her.

I grabbed the sled and started the job of getting Melissa on top of it. It was a lot harder than I imagined as I had to brace the sled while I was maneuvering her. My persistence paid off and within a few minutes I was walking down the path with the sled sliding along mostly on its own right behind me.

I actually passed the turn to the house and only discovered my mistake when I realized there were no tracks or footprints visible on the snow. I turned around and found the turn just a few yards behind me. The sled tracks were getting harder and harder to follow and I found myself retracing my own footprints that now seemed easier than the tracks to see.

After walking for a while, I started to panic as I couldn't see the lights of the house. We were now heading into the wind and forward visibility was practically zero. Finally, the tracks led us around whatever had been blocking our view and the house appeared before us. It was a mystical sight, lights in the darkness as seen through an almost blinding blizzard.

I picked up my pace. I dreaded going back into the house but it was that or die for sure out here in the snow. As we came within a few yards of the house I could see a police vehicle, it looked like one of the sheriff's cars, in the driveway. The driver's door was open and the lights inside of the car were on. I didn't see anyone inside the car.

I was tempted to just go to the vehicle but knew the deputies had to be in the house so I decided to go into the house instead. Pulling the sled up to the side door that I used to leave the house earlier, I started talking again to Melissa is an effort to get her to some state of consciousness.

"Melissa, wake up, we need to go inside and warm up. The police are here. Everything is going to be all right." I shook her a little and kept talking. She moaned and tried to push me away. Good sign, I thought.

She finally responded and I was able to slowly get her to her feet. We staggered together through the door and entered the house. It was quiet.

"Hello," I called out. No response.

"No, no, not here!" Melissa had figured out where I brought her.

"It's ok, the police are here and Benny is gone. I will take care of you, remember?"

"No, let me go," she continued to struggle, but I put my arm around her and started walking towards the entrance to the kitchen. She moved reluctantly with me.

I couldn't blame her for not wanting to be back here. I didn't either but there was nowhere else to go and we couldn't stay outside. The only other nearby place would have been the Acorn's, but with the conditions as they were, I didn't think I could have found their house. This was the only place that we had a chance to get to and I felt extremely lucky we even made it here.

Still, now that we were here, I shared her dread of being here. I just wanted to make contact with the deputies and get the hell away. We turned into the kitchen while I was still trying to comfort Melissa. She saw him before I did and let out a stifled scream. I looked and saw him. A sheriff's deputy, one I had not met before, sitting on the floor against the cabinets with his throat cut ear to ear. A large pool of blood covered his torso and pooled in the area between his legs.

"Damn," was all I could say, instinctively crouching and looking around. Melissa crouched down with me, part as a reflex and part because I never let go of her. I didn't see anything and all was still quiet.

I stood back up.

"Stay here," I whispered to Melissa. But she looked at me like I was the one crazy and grabbed hold of my wrist. She wouldn't let go. The sight of the dead deputy had gotten rid of the haziness in her mind.

"Okay, stay close, be quiet, and let go of me."

She let go of my wrist, but I could feel her hand on the

back of my sweatshirt. We walked to the front hallway. There was nobody in the hallway or in the portion of the living room that we could see to our left. I turned right toward the front door. We saw the second deputy as soon as we reached the doorway to the study. He was lying face down in the study with a nasty stab wound to the base of his neck. Melissa tensed and I could hear a soft whimper but that was all.

I looked at her and raised my finger to my lips. "Shh."

I moved closer to the body. I wanted to know if he was alive and I was worried it might be Peter. He wasn't Peter and I didn't think he was alive. I looked out the window at the police car and the hairs on the back of my neck tried to make their final desperate attempt to pull themselves out and flee. The door to the car was now shut and the lights inside were off.

She was still here. I looked around and saw a phone. I drew Melissa with me over to it and picked up the receiver. It still had a dial tone, I dialed 911. The phone rang twice and a woman answered. I cut her off and said to send the police immediately, that at least two deputies had been killed and that I had found Melissa Ribbons.

"May I have your name and location, please?"

I was about to answer the 911 operator when I heard her.

"Benny, is that you, are you back? You know not to track snow through the house. Benny?"

I could see the snow that had fallen from our shoes and clothes melting and making a nice trail down the hall to the study. Melissa backed up and cowered against the wall.

Then she appeared.

"Oh, I thought you were Benny." She stood there in the hallway at the entrance to the study. She still had on the party dress, but now it was streaked with blood. Her right arm was covered with blood from the elbow to her hand, a hand that tightly gripped the large nasty looking knife that was used a little while ago to cut the birthday cake and then kill two men, maybe more.

I felt like I was getting sick. I wanted to sit down. It was like I had just finished a marathon and was now being told that I had to keep running. I hadn't eaten since breakfast, was still half frozen, could no longer use my left arm and here I was staring at a two hundred and fifty pound, insane woman holding a big bloody knife.

"Benny will be here in a few minutes, Prissy." I hated the odds and just wanted to stall.

"Who are you calling?"

I had forgotten I was still holding onto the receiver.

"A towing company, I'll need some help getting my car back to town."

"Hang the phone up."

I did so. I knew that every 911 operator in the country could immediately trace calls and that if the call was interrupted their procedure was to send out someone to check. My concern wasn't that no one would come, it was how long would it take in this weather to get someone here.

"Jackie, go back to your room." Prissy said ominously. "I need to talk to Jim in private."

"Don't go anywhere, Melissa. Prissy, you better check out back for Benny. I don't know why he isn't back yet, but he may have gotten lost. Why don't you go on out back and see if you can find him? He may need you."

"Benny doesn't need any help. He knows this area like the back of his hand. He doesn't need any help."

"You would feel awful bad if he was lost and you didn't

try to help. You know you would."

"My Benny told me it was a bad idea to invite you to the party. Something tells me I should have listened to him." She looked over at Melissa and then back at me. "You went and took her away from her Daddy, didn't you? He said he didn't trust you with her and you went and stole her away anyway didn't you?"

She again looked at Melissa. "Jackie, darling, did this man take advantage of you? Did he force himself on you?"

Melissa stood there, visibly shaking. She didn't say anything but shook her head.

"Don't worry, baby, you don't have to talk in front of him. Now go to your room."

Melissa stayed still.

"Now!" Prissy screamed.

"Melissa, stay where you are," I said, trying to sound more confident than I felt. I looked out the window hoping to see the lights of a police car heading up the road. All I could see was darkness.

"Arghh!" Prissy screamed and charged at me with the knife held high above her ahead.

I stood still, like the proverbial deer in the headlights, wanting her to think I was an easy target. I needed her to continue this classic attack as the defense against it was one of the first taught anyone in a self defense class.

She was faster than I expected but her approach was predictable. She charged in and slashed down. At the last second, I stepped in and across with my right leg, grabbing her right arm and pulling her down and over my right hip. Her momentum carried her more than I did and she went tumbling over me into a small coffee table and crashing into the wall. Unfortunately, she never let go of the knife.

I turned to Melissa and yelled at her to run. She didn't move but it didn't matter as Prissy was already back up on her feet snarling and dripping spittle out of her mouth. She charged me again, this time with both arms extended horizontally. She wanted to grab me, pull me in and start stabbing.

I backed up a couple of steps and tried slipping quickly under her left arm to evade her grasp. She reacted quickly and while I did escape her clutch she spun and slashed at me with the knife, hacking a chunk of flesh out of my left arm just above the elbow.

I kept trying to circle her to keep her off balance, but she just moved to her left and cut me off. I took a step back and she charged again. I took another step back to give myself room to focus on grabbing her knife hand but caught the edge of the couch. I lost my balance and fell backwards. She was all over me before I hit the ground. I grabbed her wrist and tried to wrench the knife out of her hand while we were both crashing backwards. I fell hard and smashed my head against something. I saw stars and then Prissy's face crunched into mine.

The world turned dark. I could feel myself fighting to stay in touch with reality but knowing all along I was slipping back into the dream world that I had spent way too much time in the last few days. This time I wanted to stay there.

Chapter 24

I felt like I was back lying in the snow. I could see the snow falling on my face. I tried licking the snow because I was thirsty, very thirsty. It tasted good. I went back to sleep.

At some point I realized I was hearing a women's voice. I tried to move but couldn't. Was it Melissa, was she okay? Then my heart stopped, I heard the voice say Jackie. Prissy!

I tried to will myself awake and fought to sit up, but strong hands pushed me back. Impervious to my struggling I knew she was restraining me. There was a sudden pain in my arm followed by a burning sensation.

"No," I moaned, not the drugs.

"It's alright, Jim." The voice taunted me.

"Bitch," was all I could manage to mumble before darkness sucked me back into its depths.

I don't know how long I laid there. I thought I could hear voices but mostly it was quiet. I had entered that semi-conscious state where I somehow knew I was dreaming but either didn't want or simply couldn't stop the dreams from happening.

I was on a small fishing boat in a lake with John and Martha Ribbons. They were dressed in mourning but I was in jeans and t-shirt. I had a fishing pole in my hands. They were just staring at me. Beyond them I could see something floating in the water. I knew what it was but didn't want to look at it. I tried turning my head but couldn't. The thing kept drifting with the current getting closer and closer. John and Martha kept staring at me. I noticed the fishing pole in my hands was small. It was a child's pole. I wanted it to slide out of my hands but I didn't dare throw it away as they kept staring at me.

The thing floating in the water kept drifting closer and closer. I couldn't move and they kept staring at me. I could feel the sweat gathering on my eyebrows and start dripping into my right eye. It burned but I didn't dare move. Suddenly there was a soft thud and the floating thing bumped the boat and moved a foot or two away. It rolled over as it did so. I started screaming and thrashing around to get off the boat as little five year old Melissa's dead eyes looked accusingly at me as her body floated quietly in the water.

I sensed time was moving on again and I just wanted to sleep.

The room was bright. I tried to cover my eyes and found I could only move my right arm and something seemed to be tied to it making movement awkward. I saw motion in the room. Someone was closing the blinds to the window. The brightness was fading away and I could start making things out. I didn't recognize my surroundings. Someone was standing by the window and there were two people sitting in chairs by a door. They seemed to be staring at me. I didn't recognize them at first but when I did I knew it was John and Martha. God, what was I going to say? My mind was spinning, I just saw them on the boat and now they were here.

"Sorry," I tried to say more but couldn't make my mouth work.

They stood up and came a step closer to me. They were

talking to each other but I couldn't understand what they were saying. One of them, Martha, left the room. John looked at me curiously.

"How do you feel?"

I noticed the other person had come around the bed and was looking at some monitors I was hooked up to. She was a nurse. I thought I recognized her, which I realized would be understandable as I had spent a lot of time in this hospital since I arrived in Ruidoso.

"I don't know." I looked down at myself. My left shoulder and arm were completely covered with bandages. Only a few inches of wrist and hand were visible. My midsection was wrapped from just above my hips to just below my heart with stretches of tape and patches of bandages. I felt the back of my head and found a bandage.

"How long have I been here?"

"Since yesterday evening."

I looked at John. I needed to ask him but I didn't want to. He looked at me seemingly understanding what was on my mind. Then he glanced at the door and with a smile spoke to me.

"I think the answer to that question has something to say to you."

I looked over at the door to see the arrival of Martha and Melissa. Martha had tears in her eyes but Melissa didn't. Melissa had already suffered and cried enough. She approached me and knelt down close to me.

"Thank you, Mr. West. Thank you so very much."

I looked at her. She was a beautiful young lady. Martha gently touched her shoulder and Melissa stood up. I marveled how good she looked. Much better in the white slacks and green turtle neck sweater than in that loathsome birthday dress.

"Any time," I said with a smile. They all smiled but who was I kidding. I never wanted to go through anything like that again in my life.

Just then a doctor came in and sent everyone but the nurse out. John said we would talk later and left the room.

The doctor was a different one than the couple I had already met. He was all work, looking at my eyes, listening to heart and lungs, reading the monitors and poking me everywhere I hurt.

"How do you feel?"

"Crappy. What all is wrong with me?"

Instead of answering me right away he asked a series of dumb questions like where I was from, what hotel I was staying at, what color was his pen, etc. Finally, he pulled up a chair and sat down next to my bed.

"In a nutshell, sir, we almost lost you last night. You lost about a pint of blood more than the textbooks say a person can lose and still stay alive. The team that worked on you last night said that you had more holes in you seeping blood than they have ever seen on a patient before. You were delirious for half the night and at one point you had to be restrained to the bed. I think the only reason you lived was because your body temperature was so low. They figured you were operating on sheer adrenalin until you blacked out."

"What happened to Mrs. Hamilton?"

"I don't know anything about what happened before you arrived at the hospital. I do know you are a bit of a celebrity. We have had calls by the press from all over the country this morning."

"Please don't let them near me."

"Don't worry. Those are the same orders we have from the District Attorney, the Police Chief and the Sheriff. In fact, now that you are awake, there are some deputies waiting downstairs that want to talk to you. By the way, you'll be here at least another two to three days. We need to make sure you are fully recovered and safely patched up before we let you leave this time."

He stood up to leave.

"Thanks Doc." I turned to the nurse, "to all of you, thanks."

The doctor left the room but the nurse stayed. I looked at my right arm and saw an IV hooked up to it. There was also some kind of monitoring device attached to my arm with wires running out to an odd piece of equipment. The nurse was busy thumping the sack of liquid attached to the IV.

I put my head back down on the pillow and must have dozed off again.

"Hey, you're supposed to be awake. Wake up or they won't let us stay in here."

I recognized the voice but it took a second to wake back up.

"Where were you guys when I needed you?"

Rick Maldonado and Peter Blanco stood there next to my bed. I could tell they may have taken my comments more seriously than I intended.

"I'm just teasing guys, seriously."

They both visibly loosened up.

"We have a million questions for you, but all but a couple can wait until tomorrow. We're mostly here to make sure you are doing okay and to tell you how happy we are that you did pull through." Rick was doing the talking but I could see Peter wanted to get a word in too.

"I should have gone with you, man." Peter said. "I was being pulled in a couple of different directions but I should have been there for you. I'm sorry."

"Don't be like that, I could have waited. There is no blame on you. What questions do you have and then I have a bunch myself."

"What happened to Mr. Hamilton? Do you know where he is?" Rick was asking the questions.

I thought for a second. "He's right where we would have found Melissa if things had gone his way, at the bottom of the ridge line probably half way between the Hamilton's and the Acorn's houses. We were fighting and he went over, almost pulled me with him. He might have survived the fall, but I doubt it. He picked the location and he wouldn't have wanted Melissa to survive it."

"Did either of them admit to killing the other girls?"

"Yes, he did. I don't think Prissy, Mrs. Hamilton, was involved in any of the killings. Of the girls, that is, she was the one that killed the two deputies. Hamilton was already dead by then and they hadn't arrived when I left the house."

"Why did they do it?" Peter asked.

"Mrs. Hamilton brought the girls home. She somehow imagined each girl was her dead daughter, Jackie, and that she had come home to celebrate her birthday. In her mind, Jackie was still alive. He knew better and ultimately just played along to keep his wife happy. The first girl, Prissy brought home the year after Jackie died, Hamilton freed right away and convinced the girl not to report it. But after that they ended up keeping the girl each year."

"They both had to be crazy." Rick stated the obvious.

"That they were. He claimed he never abused any of the girls but I don't know if he was telling the truth. How is

Melissa doing? I mean I saw her just a little while ago and she looked okay, but how is she?"

"Physically she's fine," Peter answered. "She just has a few bruises to her face where she was probably slapped or punched a few times, nothing broken though. She had a nasty contusion on the back of her head but a couple of stitches fixed her right up."

"Our biggest concern," Rick added, "is her emotional and mental health after going through something like that. But, since there apparently wasn't any sexual abuse or other extreme physical abuse, the doctors here at the hospital tell me she should be able to effectively readjust to normal life over time."

Peter finished the commentary. "They have a couple of psychiatrists here at the hospital that spent all morning with her and she has been assigned a counselor who will work with her until the family goes back to Florida."

"Your questions?" Rick asked.

"How did I end up here? And, what happened to Mrs. Hamilton?"

"You don't know?" Peter asked before he realized that it was a rather dumb question. "I thought you knew. She's dead, stabbed right through the heart with her own knife. We thought you stabbed her. That's what Melissa thought too. She said that you two were fighting over the knife."

"We were but the last thing I remember was falling backwards and she was falling right on top of me. She must have fallen on the blade. I don't remember ever getting the knife from her."

"Well either way she is dead and no one feels sorry for her. Melissa thought you were both dead and called 911. Deputies had already been dispatched there because of the first call, which you made, right?"

"Yes, I think so."

"The 911 operator kept Melisa talking on the phone until we could get people out there. The weather was ferocious last night but fortunately we had a vehicle already in the area. The first report that came in from the 911 response team was that they thought they had four dead people and one survivor. In addition to your blood, you were covered in a lot of Mrs. Hamilton's blood as she was sprawled partly on you."

Rick jumped back into the conversation. "Despite the weather we must have ended up with over twenty law enforcement and medical people out there within the hour. By then, of course everyone knew you were alive and we were trying to keep you that way."

I looked at Rick, "You were out there last night?"

"We both were," he replied. "There is a forensic team still out there. The FBI is there now, too. Officially they are just supporting us, but my guess is that before the day is out they will have assumed the lead in the case."

"You know how you feds are," Peter jibed, "you always like to wait until the case is solved before you step in."

An older looking nurse, who I recognized as the one who picked on me a day or two earlier for wearing the slippers, came in.

"You all need to leave now," she said addressing Rick and Peter. "Come back later this evening, if you want, but Mr. West needs to get his rest."

"Okay," Rick responded. "The only pressing issues we had were the whereabouts of Hamilton and the connection with the other girls. What you told us will enable us to focus our efforts. The snow has stopped so we should be able to find Hamilton."

"I'll stop back by this evening, Jim," Peter announced as he was walking out.

"Me, too, so get some rest." Rick waved as he left.

As they left, the nurse looked out the door to make sure they were actually leaving. She then turned with a conspiratorial look on her face.

"I wanted them to leave. They can talk to you later. The doctor does want you to rest and I have a more important visitor who wants to see you for a few minutes. So I needed those two gone so we can get in one more person before we close your door to any visitors for a while."

I was a little confused about what she was actually trying to say until she stepped out of the room and returned within seconds with Kristi. She ushered Kristi in and then closed the door behind her. Kristi was carrying a vase of flowers.

"I hope you don't mind that I brought you these," she said holding out the flowers.

I didn't mind. "You look great," I said. "Come sit down," and motioned to the chair next to the bed. "I guess I stood you up again, last night. Sorry."

"I did wonder what you had gotten yourself into. When I first found out about what happened, maybe eight o'clock last night, they weren't sure if you were going to make it. I tried to come down and see you, but they wouldn't let me. I'm just so happy you are going to be okay."

"Me, too."

"Everyone is so proud of you for rescuing Melissa. Oh, and Rose told me to tell you not to worry about your room. They'll keep your things undisturbed and not bill you for last night, tonight or as long as you have to spend in here."

I felt like saying that was the last thing on my mind, but I knew everyone was just trying to be nice.

Kristi continued, "I had a chance to speak to Melissa just a few minutes ago. She was with her parents down the hall. She seems fine, but I know she must be shaken up."

Kristi stretched her arm over and gently took hold of my left hand. "The nurse said that you are in stable condition. Now that they have you patched up, you will just be here a few days. So I'm going to hold you to our dinner date, no more excuses. We'll just have to schedule it a few days from now when you have your strength back."

"Will I need it?"

"I think you might. And something else, no more detective work or whatever you do for a while. You need to rest."

We talked for a while about the gang at the restaurant. She said they all wanted to hear firsthand what happened so she could wait until then too. That was fine by me I was really tired of talking about anything by then. I was happy just to have her there beside me.

A soft knock at the door interrupted us. A different nurse opened the door and peaked through and asked me if the Ribbons family could come in for a second.

"Sure," I answered and asked Kristi to stay.

Father, mother and daughter all entered.

"Jim," John said once they were all in, "we just got permission to take Melissa back to the hotel with us, so we are going to take off. I understand you will be here for at least one more night, so I'll come tomorrow to spend some time with you."

"That's fine, enjoy the day. We'll chat tomorrow."

"One thing, though, Melissa wants to have a picture taken with you, is it all right?"

"Absolutely."

Melissa came around and Kristi started to get up to get out of the picture.

"No stay," instructed Melissa.

Both parents concurred and Kristi sat back down.

"In fact, why don't you two get in the picture, too, and I'll take the picture." The nurse suggested and Melissa reinforced.

In a minute, I had the four of them bunched around me and all smiling as the nurse took two pictures with John's camera and then one with her cell phone.

Martha and Melissa quickly inspected and approved the pictures despite comments like 'does my hair really look like that?'

"Thanks, Jim," John said as they were all walking out, "tomorrow."

"Tomorrow," I responded with a half wave.

"They seem like nice people," Kristi remarked.

"They are."

We talked some more until I must have fallen asleep, as the last thing I remember was Kristi sitting there beside me. When I opened my eyes, the nurse that was in my room earlier that day with the doctor was leaning over me peeling bandages off to inspect the early progress on my various wounds.

She was attractive and I was just thinking that it wouldn't be so bad to stay here another day or two, when she realized I was awake and watching her.

"Oh, I didn't mean to wake you. I was just making sure all the stitches and bandages were staying put and doing their job."

"Are they?"

"So far so good."

"How about all the other readings, am I going to live?" I joked but I was curious.

"Everything is looking more normal. None of your injuries were life threatening by themselves. Cumulatively and with all the blood you lost, however, put you in critical status for a long while last night. The other thing we want to keep an eye out for now is infection. So far so good, but infections happen too frequently and can be deadly. Bottom line, if everything continues as they are now you should be good to go in a day or two. Oh, you'll be sore for quite a while. You will need some follow up visits and possibly some physical therapy but there will be no need to keep you here."

When she left, my dinner arrived. There wasn't much there and eating only served to make me realize how hungry I really was.

Peter and Rick showed up just after dinner and I sent Peter out to find a vending machine. He came back with a Diet Coke and a large Butterfinger and I munched and sipped while we talked.

A cursory look for Hamilton's body revealed nothing, but a more extensive effort was planned for the next morning. Several items of clothing were found in the Hamilton's residence that they believed belonged to the earlier victims. One thing that I hadn't thought of was also discovered, a series of peep holes that allowed someone to watch what was going on inside Jackie's bedroom, bathroom and closet. We discussed whether the holes were just so both Hamilton's could keep an eye on their victim or if Benny Hamilton was a voyeur. We left that as a toss-up. The fact was that neither would be using the peep holes again.

I walked them through my whole story from finding my car battery dead to fighting Prissy Hamilton. They spent an hour hashing over every last detail with me and capturing it on tape. There would be no prosecution but they still needed to go back to four families and let them know that their daughters' deaths were not accidents.

I knew for some it might be welcomed as closure but for others it would be like opening an old wound. I was just glad that I didn't have to do it.

Over the next day and a half nothing much happened as far as I was concerned. I had a series of visitors from the town, even Marge showed up decked out to impress. She admitted that she understood that Kristi may have a little edge on her but told me not to forget her if I just felt like getting away for a while.

John Ribbons came and spent about an hour with me talking about old times. It was awkward. I knew he felt guilty about putting me through this while at the same time couldn't thank me enough. He wanted to pay me something, anything he had said. But I didn't want anything. I hadn't done this for pay. I had done it out of friendship. It was nice seeing him but I was glad when he left.

Kristi and I spent a lot of time talking and had pretty much agreed to spend some time together after I got out. I pressed her to let me take her to South Padre, Texas, for a week or maybe on a cruise and she tentatively agreed. I was feeling pretty good by the time they released me from the hospital just before lunch.

I hadn't seen Kristi that morning and had expected to. There was no call from her so I decided to walk back to the hotel. I was wearing the new pair of jeans, new flannel shirt and a new, replacement jacket for Larry. All of which Kristi had purchased and brought to me the night before as I no longer had any clothes left worth wearing.

As I walked out of the front door of the hospital I was met by Sharon Cane, the Chief of Police's secretary.

"Jim, Jim" she was calling me from the parking lot as she walked quickly to me. "Jim, I have something for you that the Captain wanted me to run over to you this morning. We were afraid you might be leaving town and wanted to get this to you."

She handed me an envelope.

"Well, thank you, what is it?"

"It's a note to you from one of the earlier victim's family. It came in an envelope Fed Ex'd to the Captain, with a note inside asking that we get it to you. The Captain thought you might like to have it now rather just mailing it to you in the future."

"That's nice of you. Please tell the captain thanks for me."

"I will. I also want you to know how happy we are that you rescued Melissa and that both of you are going to be okay."

I thanked her again for bringing me the note. She turned to go back to her car and I started walking towards the Mescalero Café putting the envelope in the jacket's inside breast pocket. The sky was a bright blue and the sun was rapidly melting the snow on the ground. I cut across the street between the Brown Bear Inn and the café. Looking at the bank I saw that the temperature was a degree above freezing. It felt a lot warmer.

As soon as I was inside the restaurant I knew something was up. There was a policeman standing at the counter talking to Larry and Daisy. Ellen was serving a table but seemed to be more interested in what was going on at the counter. There was no sign of Kristi in the room.

I walked over to Larry. "Excuse me Larry, is Kristi here?"

All three turned and looked at me. I could see Daisy had tears in her eyes.

"She's gone, Jim, she left this morning, nobody knows where."

"What do you mean, Daisy?"

The police officer interrupted briefly. "Excuse me Larry, Daisy. I'll call you when I find out anything. Please let me know if you hear from her, too, or if he shows up." He turned, nodded at me and walked out of the café.

Daisy grabbed me by the hand and led me to the closest table. "Larry, bring us some coffee and the paper, and the note." Larry turned to do what he was told.

Daisy, still holding my hand, looked back at me and said, "It's her ex."

"What? How did he find her?"

"Oh, let me grab that paper." She got up walked over to the counter and grabbed a newspaper. She got back to the table just seconds before Larry did with the coffee. He had three cups and joined us at the table.

"This is what caused the trouble." She displayed a page in the paper that contained the picture taken in my hospital room of Melissa and her parents, Kristi and me. The article identified all of us. There was only brief mention of Kristi but it mentioned she was employed at the Mescalero Café.

"A call came in here at eight this morning for Kristi. It was a man. I didn't think anything of it and just gave her the phone. A few minutes later when I looked back at her she was as white as a sheet. The phone was down by her side but she was still holding it. She told me it was him, her ex. Somehow he saw the picture and was driving down to talk to her. He said he would be here by lunch time and that he was going to take her back with him to Lubbock. I knew she was upset so I asked Larry to take her to the police station to make a report."

"I told her I would," Larry joined in the conversation. "She said she needed a few minutes to pull herself together and went to the back room. She never came out. I finally went in to look for her but she had gone out the back door."

"At first we thought something had happened to her, she wasn't answering her cell." Daisy had taken over the conversation again. "We called the police and they sent someone over here to talk to us. While the police were here, Kristi called. She said she was okay but that she had to go away for a while. She wouldn't say where she was going but that she thought after a few months she might be able to come back. She absolutely does not want her ex to ever see her again. I know she's terrified of him."

"Where did she say she was going?" I asked.

"She didn't. She said she would let us know once she was safe somewhere but that was all. She said not to hold her job, but that she hoped at some point to earn it back. I think she was crying when she said good bye."

"Has anyone been to her place?"

"Yes, but no one answered the bell. The police finally got inside but she was not there."

"There was this note for you, Jim," Larry added.

It was the second time that day I received an envelope addressed to me and this one was placed with the other. They both looked at me. I knew they wanted me to read it and share it with them. I wasn't going to.

"Has anyone seen this ex of hers? Do we even know if he is coming? He may have just been harassing her?"

"No, no one has come here asking for Kristi. We don't know what he looks like. The police are trying to find out where he is at this moment. They think he was just bluffing. But it doesn't matter, like Larry said, she's gone."

"I wish she didn't leave like that." I said more angrily than I should have been.

"You really like her, don't you?" Daisy asked.

"Yes, I do," I admitted. "I wanted to get to know her a lot better, too. Why is she letting this guy continue to mess up her life?" It was a rhetorical question. I didn't expect an answer and didn't get one. "If you hear from her will you let me know? Tell her I want to see her. That I can help. I'll be here in town tonight, but tomorrow if she is still gone I'll probably be heading home."

"Sure," answered Daisy.

I got up and walked out. I was back in my motel room before I realized I didn't pay for the coffee or give Larry his new jacket. I laid down on the bed to think but just fell asleep. I didn't dream and woke up at five when the phone rang.

"Hey Jim, how are you doing?" It was Peter. I told him I felt surprisingly better than I would have thought just a couple of days after being shot and almost dying.

"I just wanted to call and tell you that if you want to head home that it's okay with the Sheriff. We have everything we need from you. Anything else we can get by deposition."

"Thanks, Peter, I'll probably head out in the morning."

"I also wanted to let you know that the doctors think that Teddy will pull through. It is still early to be sure and he may have some brain damage but they think he'll live."

"I guess that may be good for the family," I said, just to say something. I really didn't care.

"The other thing, man, if I can ever do anything for you, let me know. I owe you big time."

I wondered if he still felt guilty about not being there when I could have used some help, especially since I had just pulled his fat out of the fire a few days earlier.

"Don't worry about it, but if I need to contact someone down here in the future for some help, I'll call you."

"Thanks," he said, "I really enjoyed getting to know you. Have a safe trip."

I hung up. It was getting dark outside and I was getting hungry. I didn't want to go back to the Café. Not with Kristi being gone. I walked down to a Mexican restaurant I had passed during my walk from the hospital.

I read and then re-read the two notes while I wolfed down a plate of enchiladas. After eating I went back to the Brown Bear Inn and sat in my room. I wasn't tired and I knew I wouldn't fall asleep.

Chapter 25

At nine I packed up my few things and checked out of the hotel. Rose was not there but I asked the old man if he would make sure Larry got the jacket and the two dollars for the coffee. He looked surprised but said he would.

I walked out into the hotel's small parking lot and found my car with its new battery. It had been towed by the city back to my hotel while I was in the hospital. It started up fine. I looked over at the sign in front of the bank. It was flashing twenty degrees. I didn't feel that cold.

My mind was on the note as I pulled out onto the road, just as it had been ever since I first read it. It wasn't the note from Kristi. Her note had been a nice one, telling me she thought she loved me and hoped one day to be able to take that cruise. She apologized for running but claimed it was the only thing she could do. She was terrified of her ex husband and she didn't want him to hurt her or any of the people that meant so much to her, especially me. She said that after a few months she thought it would be safe to contact me and she said she would.

I knew she was doing what she thought was necessary but I found the whole thing frustrating. I would never have recommended running as the solution. Besides, I had fallen for her like I had fallen only once or twice since my divorce. Each time, like now, something took that relationship away from me and I didn't like it. She had made her decision. All

I could do now was to see how it played out.

The sign that notified drivers that they were leaving Ruidoso whizzed by me on my right. Roswell was still an hour away and Clovis even further but I knew fatigue wouldn't be a problem tonight.

My mind still had to come to terms with the second note. It was a simple one, but it was one that I knew would keep me awake for quite a while. The note was from the twins who were sisters of Hamilton's third victim. The victim with the red stocking cap embroidered with a gold star. The victim whose hat was still sitting in the hall closet. It wasn't even so much the note itself as it had been quite straightforward.

'Dear Sir,' the note had started. 'My twin sister and I wanted to write you a short note to thank you for finding out what really happened to our sister and in bringing justice to her murderers. Ever since her disappearance and discovery we both have been troubled with the way it had ended. We both have had strong feelings that something wasn't right and that Stephanie couldn't rest until the truth came out. Both of us woke up this morning feeling like a load had been lifted off us. Later when we received the call from the police and learned about what you had done, we realized that Stephanie could now rest in peace. We know this sounds silly but it meant a lot to us and we wanted to write and thank you. We have enclosed a picture of Stephanie as we knew she would want you to have it.'

It was the picture, not the actual note that I knew would stay with me forever. The picture was taken at fairly close range and depicted Stephanie running at the camera. She was wearing an all white jogging suit and had on the red hat. She was smiling and her eyes looked right at you. On the side of the picture was just written the word "Thanks!"

I recognized the photo right away as my phantom jogger who had led me out of the forest that night. The jogger whom I could still see clearly in my mind, but had readily accepted as being a figment of my imagination. The jogger who saved my life allowing me to keep going in my effort to save Melissa and in the process, solve the mystery of her own death.

The picture was in the envelope on the seat next to me but I could still see it vividly in my mind. The picture had said thanks. I drove on, toward the rising moon. "No," I heard myself saying, "thank you."

Author Bob Doerr

Bob Doerr grew up in a military family, attended the Air Force Academy, and then had a career of his own in the Air Force. It was a life style that had him moving every three or four years, but also one that exposed him to the people and cultures of numerous countries in Asia, Europe and to most of these United States. In the Air Force, Bob specialized in criminal investigations and counterintelligence gaining significant insight to the worlds of crime, espionage and terrorism. In addition to his degree from the Academy he also has a Masters in International Relations from Creighton University. Bob now lives in Garden Ridge, Texas, with his wife of 36 years and their pet dog.

To find out about new titles, release dates, book signings, speaking engagements and other appearances visit

www.bobdoerr.com

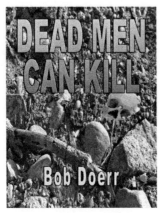

- **Title:** *Dead Men Can Kill*
- **Author: Bob Doerr**
- **Price: $27.95**
- **Publisher: TotalRecall Publications, Inc.**
- **Format: HARDCOVER, 6.14" x 9.21"**
- **Number of pages: 320**
- **13-digit ISBN:** 978-1-59095-758-5
- **Publication: December 8, 2009**

When Jim West, a former Air Force Special Agent with the Office of Special Investigations, moves back to New Mexico, his goal is simple: start an easy going second career as a professional lecturer on investigative techniques to colleges and civic organizations. He never envisioned that his practical demonstration of forensic hypnosis on stage with a state university student would stir up memories of an 18-year old murder mystery. When the student is murdered three days later, West finds himself ensnared in a web of intrigue that pits him and the small town's authorities against a ruthless, psychotic killer.

An aggressive reporter for the town newspaper seeks out West for help with the story, but after one of her co-workers is murdered, she quickly aligns her efforts with West and the Sheriff. As West works closely with her, he begins to wonder if this could be the first real relationship for him since his devastating divorce a few years earlier.

The killer, though, has other plans for the reporter and the story takes fascinating twists and turns, leading to an inevitable, riveting confrontation.

Advance Praise

Look out for a new hero on the mystery/thriller landscape! Jim West, retired military investigator, is resourceful, intuitive, pragmatic and always competent. All of West's abilities are tested when he matches wits with psychopathic serial killer William White, a man whose appreciation for murder is surpassed only by his delight in domination. Bob Doerr has crafted a must-read addition to the genre in Dead Men Can Kill, which evolves from absorbing story to absolute page-turner as West closes in on a killer who is supposedly dead. Highly recommended!

     --Dallin Malmgren, author of...
     The Whole Nine Yards   The Ninth Issue   Is This for a Grade?

A Jim West™ Mystery/Thriller

LaVergne, TN USA
10 December 2009

166513LV00004B/1/P